Two-Minute Drill

Two-Minute Drill

a Comeback Kids novel

MIKE LUPICA

SCHOLASTIC INC.
New York Toronto London Auckland Sydney
Mexico City New Delhi Hong Kong Buenos Aires

ISBN-13: 978-0-545-09465-8
ISBN-10: 0-545-09465-8

12 11 10 9 8 7 6 5 4 3 2 1   8 9 10 11 12 13/0

Printed in the U.S.A.   40

First Scholastic printing, September 2008

Design by Gina DiMassi
Text set in Bookman

Once more, this book is for
my amazing wife, Taylor,
and our four amazing children,
Chris, Alex, Zach and Hannah.
I tell them here what I tell them a lot:
No one is luckier than I am.

ACKNOWLEDGMENTS

Christopher Dykes, M.A., C.A.S. He is the school psychologist at Saxe Middle School, New Canaan, Conn., and proved as I wrote this book that he's never afraid to take on a new student. No matter how old that student is. And Coach Green, as always.

Two-Minute Drill

There were a lot of bad pa. that came with being the new kid.

Scott Parry was already used to eating by himself at lunch, having nobody to talk to yet at recess.

And after just four days in the sixth grade at Bloomfield South, he pretty much expected to be sitting by himself on the short bus ride home.

He had always been shy, even in his old school, in his old town. And in the school and town before that. He just hadn't realized that his new school was going to be this shy *back*.

It wasn't that Scott wasn't trying to fit in.

When they broke off into discussion groups, he tried to get with a new group of kids every time, hoping that at least one of them might want to talk to him when they were finished. And he knew better than to raise his hand every single time he knew the answer in class. But that was hard for him, because he basically knew the answer to any question his teachers asked.

It had been the same way for him at all his schools.

Sometimes he wished he weren't so smart, because it seemed to make the other kids mad. What he really wanted was to be a little less good in class and a lot more good at sports, football especially. But that's not the way things had worked out for him.

He knew teachers always liked the smart kids better, despite how they tried to act like they were treating every student the same. But he didn't want the teachers to like him. He wanted the other kids to like him. Girls or boys.

So he tried not to act like he was showing off, even though his hand still shot up more than anybody else's in sixth grade.

It's true that Scott felt alone most of the time,

like he was hiding in plain sight, but he knew he could handle being the new kid one more time.

What he couldn't handle was what happened to him every single day while he waited for the bus home.

Because Jimmy Dolan, one of the biggest kids in his class and easily the meanest, was always waiting, too. Which meant that Jimmy had plenty of time to rag on Scott every day.

Scott wanted kids at Bloomfield South to talk to him.

Just not this kid.

The only kid in the whole school that Scott didn't want talking to him or hanging with him wouldn't leave him alone.

"Hey," Jimmy Dolan said now, "here comes the brain."

Just by watching the pickup touch football games at recess—nobody had picked Scott yet, not one time—he knew Jimmy Dolan was a good football player. At recess that day, Scott had overheard a couple of the teachers talking about how Jimmy's dad was going to be the coach of the sixth-grade town team this season.

Mr. Burden, their science teacher, had said, "Maybe his father can control him."

Just then one of the smaller sixth-graders had caught a pass and even though it was supposed to be two-hand touch, Jimmy had managed to send the kid flying.

"I wouldn't count on that," Mrs. Graham, their math teacher, had said.

Waiting for the bus now, Scott tried to ignore Jimmy, tried to act as if he were searching for something really important inside his backpack.

But he knew he was wasting his time, that you had about as much chance of ignoring Jimmy Dolan as you did a stomachache.

"What's the matter, brain? You don't want to talk to me today?"

Scott had his backpack on the ground and was kneeling over it. But Jimmy was right over him, blocking out the sun like a giant black cloud.

Scott leaned to his right a little, trying to see

past Jimmy's legs, hoping the buses were starting to board.

They weren't.

"What're you looking for in there?" Jimmy said. "Maybe I can help you."

"No," Scott said. "I'm fine."

Too late.

Jimmy reached down and scooped up Scott's backpack like he was trying to beat him to a dollar he'd seen on the ground. And before Scott could do anything to stop him, Jimmy had dumped everything out on the ground.

Scott didn't care about any of the school stuff in there, his pens and notebooks and textbooks, so much stuff that his mother always asked if he was carrying bricks.

None of that mattered.

The picture mattered.

The picture of Scott's dog, Casey. Jimmy Dolan spotted it right away.

Scott tried to reach down and grab it, but once again Jimmy was too quick for him.

"Who's this?" Jimmy said. "Your girlfriend?"

"Give it back," Scott said, quieter than he wanted to.

"You carry a picture of your *dog* with you, brain?" Jimmy said, loud enough for every kid still waiting for a bus to hear. "That's like something the little nerd in that *Lassie* movie would do, right?"

Scott felt like this was some kind of assembly now, and he and Jimmy were up on stage in front of the whole school. If the other kids at Bloomfield South didn't know the new kid before this, they sure would now.

If I'm such a brain, Scott thought, *how come I can't think of a way to get myself out of this?*

As a last resort, he actually tried being nice, as hard as that was.

"Can I please have my picture back?" he said.

Jimmy smiled and shook his head no, waving the picture back and forth in front of Scott's face.

Scott lunged for it, trying to catch Jimmy by surprise.

Only he wasn't big enough. Or quick enough.

As he landed, Jimmy stuck out a leg and tripped

him, giving him a little shove on the way down for good measure.

Scott went down hard, landing on knees and elbows.

All he could hear now was laughter.

Until he heard this: "Cut it out, Dolan."

Not a teacher's voice. Not a voice belonging to any grown-up. A kid, definitely.

Scott picked himself up and saw that it was Chris Conlan.

You only had to be at Bloomfield South for one day to know that even though Jimmy Dolan was one of the bigger football players in the sixth grade, Chris Conlan was the best.

Chris Conlan wasn't just the quarterback, he was the boy all the other boys in their class wanted to be.

"What's the problem, Chris? I was just playing—"

"Give him back his picture."

Scott could see by the look on Jimmy's face how much he didn't want to back down.

"Why're you standing up for him?" Jimmy said,

sounding whiny all of a sudden. "You don't even know this guy."

"I know you, though," Chris said. "And I know you're acting like a tool. Now, for the last time, give him back his picture."

And, to Scott's amazement, Jimmy Dolan did just that.

TWO

It was like a play Chris had called in the huddle.

Jimmy handed the picture back to Scott, saying, "Whatever. Take your stupid picture."

Then he walked away shaking his head, maybe for once knowing what it felt like to look bad in front of the other kids.

"I've got a dog, too," Chris said to Scott. Then he grinned and said, "But pictures sort of don't do him justice."

"Thanks for doing that," Scott said. He stuck the picture of Casey inside his math book, started putting the rest of his books back inside the pack.

"Don't worry about it," Chris said. "He was acting stupid."

Scott smiled for the first time since school had

let out. Maybe the first time since he'd showed up at Bloomfield South on Monday morning. "I don't think he was acting," he said.

Now it was Chris's turn to smile. "He's actually not such a bad guy," he said.

"Could've fooled me."

Chris said, "It's just that the only thing he's really good at is knocking people down, like in football. And sometimes he forgets the game's over. Or hasn't started yet."

Then, as if he'd remembered something, Chris stuck out his hand.

"I'm Chris," he said.

It felt funny, and Scott was sure it looked funny, a couple of sixth-graders shaking hands, but they did it.

"I know who you are," Scott said.

"And I know who you are," Chris said. "The smartest kid in our class."

"No way."

"Way," Chris said. "Like *way* the smartest. I watch you in class sometimes when somebody else is answering, and I can just tell you know the answer."

Scott said, "Maybe that makes you the smart one."

Chris gave him a funny look.

Just then the bus line finally started to move. Scott said he'd better get going, thanked Chris one last time.

"Dolan won't bother you anymore," Chris said.

"I wish."

Chris grinned. "You're cool now," the coolest kid in their class said. "I got you."

"Well . . . cool," Scott said, because he couldn't think of anything else to say.

He started to walk toward the bus, and Chris walked with him, saying, "Hey, maybe we could hang out sometime, or whatever."

"Yeah," Scott said, "anytime."

He said it like it was no big deal, but what he really wanted to do was yell "Yeah!" and pump his fist windmill-style, the way Tiger Woods did after he sank a big putt in *Tiger Woods PGA Tour '07*.

"See you tomorrow then," Chris said.

"Yeah," Scott said again.

He had to keep himself from running up the steps to bus number three.

Flying.

Just like that, he had a friend.

THREE

His mom was waiting for him when he got home.

This was the third time they had moved in the past five years. His dad worked as a salesman for Titleist golf balls, and the more he sold, the bigger his job seemed to get. Every time it got bigger, they moved.

But no matter where they were living, one thing hadn't changed:

Scott Parry couldn't think of a day in his entire life when he'd walked into whatever house they were living in and his mom hadn't been there.

And ever since they'd gotten Casey, his golden retriever, as a pup two years ago, Casey was right there with her.

It was Casey who greeted him first today, jumping on him the minute he came through the front door, as if to say, *Where have you been all day?*

His mom was right behind, asking how school had gone, the way she did every day, the way she probably would until he stopped being the new kid.

Whenever that was.

Usually he'd just tell her fine and go straight to the cookies. But today he surprised her.

"Crazy," he said.

"Good crazy or bad crazy?" His mom was small, the way he was, and smart about practically everything. If that wasn't enough, people said Scott looked like her, too.

They were in the kitchen. It wasn't a special occasion that Scott could think of, but there on the table was what she called her Amazing Chocolate Cake.

"Both," Scott said, and then told her everything that had happened with Jimmy and Casey's picture and Chris Conlan.

"You've mentioned this Chris before," she said, "right?"

"Mom," he said, "he's the *man.*"

"And he stood up for you this way in front of all the other kids?"

"Like I said, crazy, right?"

"Doing the right thing is never crazy," his mom said. "Young Mr. Conlan doing what he did, well, that just says to me if he hadn't, that would have been crazy."

"Mom," he said, "you're the brain around here."

She smiled at him. "Don't tell your father."

"Maybe it's going to be okay at this school after all," Scott said.

He was already tearing into the huge piece of Amazing Chocolate Cake she'd cut for him. When he looked up, she was still smiling at him.

"You think?" she said.

Then she said, "You know, if you want, I could call Chris's mom . . ."

"No," Scott said. "*No, no, no.*"

"A mouthful of cake and a mouthful of no," she said.

"No," he said.

"Sorry," she said. "Got carried away there."

"Runaway Mom," Scott said.

"Leaving the kitchen now," she said, backing away. "You and Case going out to play ball when you finish eating?"

Scott smiled at her now. "If the dog doesn't practice," he said, "how's he going to get better at football?"

"You make a good point," she said, smiling.

There were woods behind their house and a pond on the other side of the woods. But between the trees and the water was a small clearing that Scott's dad made sure was mowed with the rest of their lawn.

"Got to take good care of your field of dreams," his dad would say.

It *was* Scott Parry's field of dreams.

This was where he would go with Casey and pretend he was a football player.

That he was one of the guys.

His dad had measured out the distances, painted an outline for an end zone, painted perfectly straight yard lines across the field that stretched out thirty yards. He'd even used the kind of chalk roller they used on tennis courts and baseball fields, so that Scott could make the lines white again when they started to fade.

The best part was at the back of the end zone. That's where the goalposts were, the ones his dad had put up himself, and the big old tire hanging from the crossbar.

The tire was Scott's target.

He would drop back and pretend he was throwing from the pocket. Or he'd roll out to his left or right, pretend he was being chased by some crazed guys on defense—a whole gang of Jimmy Dolans— and give himself points if one of his passes connected anyplace on the tire.

But the biggest victory, the pretend-the-crowd-goes-wild victory, was reserved for when he somehow threw the ball through the opening without touching anything, like a game-winning swish in basketball as the clock runs out. It didn't happen very often, but Scott kept trying. He blamed his lack of accuracy on the size of his hands. They were too small to get a good grip on the ball or to throw a tight spiral except by accident.

He kept practicing, anyway.

"It's what you do in sports, whether you're the star of the team or somebody at the end of the bench," his dad always told him. "You keep trying."

"Even if I grow," Scott would say to his dad sometimes, "I'll never be as good at football as you were."

"Be as good as *you* can be, kiddo," his dad would say, "and I'll be one happy guy."

Scott would throw until his arm got tired, and Casey, who never got tired, would keep tearing after the ball and bringing it back to him, holding it by one of the seams that had come loose.

And then it was time for Scott Parry to get around to the only thing he was really good at in football.

He'd kick.

He might not have the hands, or the arm, or the size.

But Scott Parry could really kick.

He'd start at the ten-yard line, which meant a twenty-yard kick, because the goalposts were ten yards deep in the back of the end zone, just like in real football, and put the ball down on the practice tee he always brought out here with him. He'd swing his leg, try to kick the ball through the uprights, pretending as hard as he could now, pretending that time was running out and the game was on the line.

Pretending that he was the best and most famous placekicker in the National Football League.

Sometimes he would put the ball on his plastic tee and pretend there were only a few seconds left in the Super Bowl.

"So it has come down to this," he'd say, like he wasn't just trying to win the game, but announce it on TV at the same time. "The whole season is on the foot of Scott Parry."

He'd take two steps back from the ball, then one long step to the left of it, take a deep breath. Then he'd stride forward and kick with everything he had, following through the way the kickers on

TV did. Sometimes he'd see how many he could make in a row from this distance, his all-time record being six.

But no matter how many he made in a row, no matter how dark it was getting or close to dinner, Scott still wasn't done for the day.

Always saving the best until last.

He had been watching with his dad the day Doug Flutie of the Patriots had made the first dropkick in the NFL in what the announcers said was like a hundred years or something. It was the last game of Flutie's long career. Scott's dad, who'd played football at Boston College with Flutie, explained how great Flutie had been when he'd played quarterback for BC, even though he was only listed at five-nine and was really shorter than that. How he'd won the Heisman Trophy, how he'd thrown one of the most famous touchdown passes in all football history against the University of Miami when he was a senior. After that, according to Scott's dad, Flutie had spent more than twenty years in pro football, in just about every league there was. Even the one in Canada.

Now Flutie was about to retire. And because it was his last game, his coach had let him try to drop-kick an extra point. It turned out Flutie loved football history almost as much as he loved playing. He knew that guys used to drop-kick all the time in the old days and had taught himself how to do it. Not only taught himself how, but gotten really good at it.

So Bill Belichick, the Patriots coach, put him in at the end of a game against the Dolphins, and Flutie drop-kicked the extra point right through. And even though that point didn't win any championships for the Patriots, his teammates had acted as if it had. So had the people in the stands that day.

"They said he was too small his whole career," Scott's dad said. "But every time anybody ever gave him a fair chance, he played as big as anybody on the field."

That was the biggest dream of all for Scott, down here behind his house, in his secret place between the woods and the water:

Someday he was going to get the chance to do something big in football.

FOUR

Chris Conlan came over on Saturday morning and brought his dog with him.

Scott hadn't asked what kind of dog it was that day when Chris had said pictures didn't do him justice. But in his head, he'd pictured a dog as big as Casey. Maybe a big old Lab, something like that.

It wasn't a Lab.

Wasn't even close.

The dog's name was Brett, Chris said, for Brett Favre, his all-time favorite quarterback.

Brett was a black-and-tan Norwich terrier.

"Wow, he's small," Scott said when Chris came walking through the front door with Brett under his arm, carrying him the way he would a schoolbook.

Chris grinned and put a finger to his lips.

"Shhhh," he said. "He *thinks* he's big."

But you had to say one thing for Brett: What he lacked in size, he made up for in speed. As soon as he was on the ground, he and Casey began tearing through every downstairs room in the house. Sometimes Casey was the one doing the chasing, sometimes Brett. Every few minutes, Casey would stop, lie down panting, tongue hanging out of the side of his mouth, and Brett would jump on his back.

The first time he did it, Chris said, "He looks like a jockey riding a horse."

"Or Stuart Little riding one," Scott said.

Right then the two dogs went tearing off again, like they were already best friends.

It wasn't long before Scott's mom pointed to them and said, "Outside. Now. Boys and dogs."

Scott couldn't wait to show Chris his field, anyway.

"Follow me," Scott said as they made their way through his backyard, "there's something you need to see."

When they came through the trees, the dogs already running ahead of them, Chris spotted the goalposts.

"This," he said, "is mad crazy."

Scott said, "Welcome to Parry Field."

Chris took Scott's football out of his hands and, without even warming up or looking as if he were putting any effort into it, threw a perfect spiral from where they were standing that nearly clipped the top of one of the uprights.

"That throw didn't exactly stink," Scott said.

"Whatever," Chris said. "Who does this field belong to?"

"Me."

"This is . . . *yours*?"

"Mine and Case's," he said. "And my dad's on weekends. You're the first . . . guy I've brought here."

He wanted to say "friend." But he stopped himself, not wanting to scare Chris the very first time they were hanging out together. Besides, he'd always thought that being friends wasn't something you talked about, it was something you just knew.

Something that just *was*.

"We gotta get some other guys from school back here as soon as possible," Chris said, his voice excited. "Have you had any games yet?"

"I don't know anybody yet," Scott said.

"Well, that's gonna change now," Chris said, like it was easy.

Maybe everything came easy to him, even being friends.

They had been so busy talking that Chris hadn't noticed Casey standing next to him, the football hanging from his mouth.

"He returned the ball?" Chris said.

Scott nodded.

Chris said, "Tell me he doesn't do that every time somebody chucks it somewhere."

"Pretty much," Scott said. "Unless he gets distracted by a squirrel or a rabbit. It's a good deal, if you don't mind a little drool."

"You throw it, and the dog goes and gets it?"

"Well, sometimes I kick it, and he goes and gets it."

"You're lucky," Chris said. "If I even try to get

Brett to fetch a ratty old tennis ball, he gives me this look, like, 'You want *me* to get that?' "

Chris and Scott started light-tossing the ball to each other then, and Casey figured out pretty quickly that he wasn't needed at the moment, so he and Brett went running off for the woods.

After a few minutes, Chris said it was time for them to cut loose a little bit and for Scott to go long.

Scott did that, running as fast as he could, feeling slower than a tractor with Chris watching him.

Chris waited until he was far enough away and put the ball right into his chest.

Scott dropped it.

"Good try," Chris yelled.

Yeah, Scott thought, maybe it's a good try if you've never played football before.

For the next few minutes, he was lucky if he caught anything. Chris kept putting the ball where he should have been able to catch it, even started taking something off his throws, lofting them a little more until they were practically like pop flies in baseball.

But the harder Scott concentrated, the harder

he tried to will the stupid ball into his hands, the worse it got. He felt clumsier than he ever had before in his life.

And more embarrassed.

The one kid in class he wanted to impress, the one kid in the whole town he wanted to impress, and he was making a total and complete idiot of himself.

It wasn't much different than if Chris had been trying to get Casey to catch the ball out of the air.

Scott thought, *I should be bringing the ball back to him in my teeth.*

"Sorry," Scott said when another pass ended up on the ground.

Chris said, "Sorry for what?"

Sounding exactly like his dad.

"I have the worst hands in the world!" Scott finally yelled.

He'd been running a pass pattern right at the goalposts, Chris had made another perfect throw, and the ball had gone off Scott's fingertips.

Casey was back now. He started to go for the ball, and Scott stopped him with, "Case? Don't even think about it."

Chris jogged over to where Scott was standing and said, "You're just trying too hard. My dad's not the greatest athlete in the world, but he always says that the thing you've got to try hardest at in sports is relaxing."

Scott managed to squeeze out a smile. "You don't understand," he said. "All I'm good at in football is trying."

He wasn't ready to tell Chris about kicking. The way things were going today, he was afraid to even put the ball on the tee, because he probably wouldn't be able to kick the ball in the water if he was standing right near the edge.

And Scott knew it was more than that.

Kicking a ball wasn't close to being as cool as what Chris could do on a football field, what he could do with a football in his hands. It was almost a different sport.

"Speaking of trying," Chris said, "are you going out for the team?"

They were standing in the middle of the field in front of the goalposts now, only a few yards apart, soft-tossing again as they talked.

But each time they did, without saying anything, Chris would take a step back. When he did, so would Scott.

"The town team? Uh, that would be a no."

Chris took two steps back now.

So did Scott.

"Come on, you gotta—it'll be great," Chris said. "And it's not really like you're trying out, anyway. They don't even call them tryouts, because if you show up and you're willing to come to practice, you're on the team. Nobody gets cut."

Chris threw a pass that had a little extra zip on it. Scott tried to concentrate as hard as he could, look the ball right into his hands the way Chris had told him to.

And dropped it.

"You're still thinking too much," Chris said.

"Because I *know* I can't play," Scott said. "Except maybe when I'm out here by myself."

By now they had the whole field between them and were shouting at each other to be heard.

"Come out for the team," Chris said. "Otherwise you're never going to find out if you're any good or not."

"I already know."

Chris's answer to that was to haul off and throw as hard a pass as he had all day, like one of those bullets the real Brett Favre would throw to one of the Packer wide receivers. The ball came in a little high, forcing Scott to jump for it, but somehow he timed the jump perfectly and looked the ball into his hands like Chris had been telling him to all day.

And made the catch.

Yes!

He felt like spiking the ball, the way guys did in the pros after they scored a touchdown, but figured he better quit while he was ahead.

"That's what I'm talking about!" Chris said. "Let's end on that one."

"Deal," Scott said.

"My mom's probably already here. See you at school."

Scott watched Chris and Brett until they disappeared into the woods, Casey following behind them, barking at Brett like he was telling him to stay, he wasn't done playing yet.

Now it was safe for Scott to kick.

No way he was going to kick in front of Chris.

He walked over to goalposts, picked up his tee where he'd left it the day before, walked back to the ten-yard line, placed the ball on the tee just right. Then he went through his little routine, measured out his two steps back and one to the side, feeling no pressure now that he was alone on the field, everything quiet back here again.

Scott took a deep breath and stepped into the kick and caught this one perfectly, kicked the ball so high and true he thought he might have made this one from thirty yards away from the posts.

As soon as the ball landed, he heard Casey barking again, so he pretended that sound was the roar of the crowd going wild.

Scott smiled, turning toward the woods as he said, "Good timing there, Case, you came back just in time to see the game-winning kick."

Only it wasn't just Casey.

Chris was there, too.

"You can *kick*?" Chris said.

He sounded shocked, but Scott didn't care. He could feel himself smiling, happy that Chris had seen him make that.

Happy and proud.

He felt like he'd really impressed him now, even more than he had with one leaping catch.

"Well, keep it to yourself," he said, trying to make it sound like the kick was no big deal.

"Don't worry," Chris said. "Your secret is safe with me."

"Oh, I get it," Scott said, "you're one of those guys who doesn't think kickers are real players."

"Not me," Chris said. "Coach Dolan."

Scott could see now that Chris wasn't joking around, he was being serious.

"Mr. Dolan doesn't like kickers?"

"He lost the Pop Warner championship for the older kids last year because a guy missed an extra point," Chris said.

Then he paused and said, "The guy *hates* kickers."

FIVE

They didn't call them tryouts here. They called them "evaluations."

Mr. Dolan, Jimmy's dad, explained this to all of them, saying that even though each and every one of them was supposed to try his hardest, they weren't trying out, because if you were willing to put in the time and the effort, you were going to be a member of his team.

Scott still thought of himself as trying out.

To him, being here meant he was trying to show he belonged, even in front of somebody like Jimmy Dolan, who'd said, "Wait a second—the brain is going to try out for *football*?" as soon as he'd seen Scott out on the field with the rest of the guys.

"Just ignore him," Chris said.

Scott kept his voice low, because the last thing he wanted to do before tryouts—evaluations—was make the coach's son mad at him. Especially *this* coach's son.

"I've got a better chance of beating you out for quarterback than I do of ignoring that guy," Scott said.

"It's gonna be fine," Chris said.

It was a disaster.

"It wasn't as bad as you think," his dad said in the car on the way home.

"You weren't there." Scott was slumped down so far in the backseat that his dad had to actually lift his head a little bit if he wanted to see him in the rearview mirror.

"As a matter of fact, champ, I was there. The whole time."

"I didn't see you."

"You weren't supposed to."

"We started at five," Scott said. "You're never home from work by then."

The evaluations had gone from five to eight, and

Scott's dad had been waiting with the other parents in the parking lot when it was over; the parents had not been allowed on the field.

"I left work early," his dad said. "And then I found a nice spot in the woods where I could watch, hoping that I wouldn't get arrested by the town football police."

"Well, if you saw us, there's no way you can think I played good," Scott said, "even if I am your son." He made a gagging sound like he was about to choke his brains out. "I was the worst one out there."

They had pulled into their driveway. Hank Parry shut off the engine but made no move to get out of the car. He just turned around so he was facing Scott. And he was smiling. Sometimes Scott would catch his dad smiling at him and have no idea why. They'd be playing football out on Parry Field, just the two of them, and Scott would be messing up all over the place the way he usually was, and still his dad would be smiling.

And Scott, no matter what was going on with him, no matter how lousy or frustrated he felt when he couldn't do anything right, would feel better looking back at him.

It was even happening now, after football evaluations that made Scott want to give himself an F.

"It was just the first night," his dad said. "You were nervous in front of the other kids, and I know you were nervous trying to impress those coaches. You think the other guys weren't feeling the same way?"

His dad was trying to make it stop hurting, basically. Scott knew that was what parents did. Well, maybe not all parents. He wasn't positive that all of them were as cool as his parents were. But his dad was acting as if Scott had just gotten knocked down and now he was trying to help him up.

He had gotten knocked down good today, no matter what kind of Band-Aid his dad was trying to put on it.

Dropped easy passes, like that was his signature move. Beaten by every kid his size in the running races. When they'd been asked to run through some tires, in what Mr. Dolan called "agility drills," he'd fallen twice his first time through.

When they were asked to do some throwing, both for distance and for accuracy, like it was one of those Pass, Punt and Kick contests, he was so bad trying to keep the ball between the ropes that Jimmy Dolan yelled out, "Hey, brain, are you sure you're right-handed?"

Everybody in earshot laughed.

Scott didn't wear a watch, so he wasn't sure what time it was, how long they'd been at it, or how many more drills he could embarrass himself in before they were finished.

But already he wanted to quit.

How come sports came so hard to him?

"I'd trade half my brain just to be half as good as some of the guys I saw out there today," he said to his dad from the backseat.

His dad still hadn't made any move to go into the house, so neither had he. He still couldn't believe his dad had come home early from work just to watch him fall all over himself in front of Jimmy Dolan's dad and the two other coaches.

"Don't ever say that," his dad said.

"Why not?"

"Because if you gave away anything from inside that amazing head of yours, you wouldn't be you," his dad said. "And I like my son just the way he is, thank you very much. Besides, I'll tell you a secret: A lot of these kids would give anything to be as smart as you."

"If I ask you something, will you tell me the truth?" Scott said.

"You know I will," his dad said. "I have a lifetime contract to do that with you."

Scott said, "Don't you wish I was better at sports than I am?"

That smile again.

His dad shook his head slowly from side to side.

"Nope," he said. "Not true. Not today. Not ever."

"Well," Scott said, "I wish I had more of you in me than I do. Like the part that made you a great football player."

"I was never great," he said. "I was all right. And then I outworked everybody enough to be better than I should have been."

But it wasn't just football with his dad. He was good at golf and tennis and swimming and softball. Everything.

Scott was good at school.

"I could outwork the whole stupid world and still not be better than *anybody*," Scott said. "I'd settle for being even a little more like you were when you were my age."

"You've got it all wrong, champ," his dad said. "Sometimes I'm the one wishing he was more like you."

"Yeah, right."

"No, I really mean it. Someday you'll be able to see what I saw today, hiding over there in the trees."

"And what's that?"

"That you were the toughest one on that field."

SIX

There were twenty-six of them who made it through to the end of practice on Wednesday night. That was the night they put on helmets and shoulder pads and real football pants and the football shoes with rubber spikes, not too different from soccer shoes, they'd been told to bring with them.

Scott knew there were twenty-six players because he'd counted them.

There had been forty when they started on Monday night. He'd counted that night, too. Now here they were, the survivors—like this was a *Survivor* show for sixth-grade football—waiting for their parents to pick them up.

He was one of the twenty-six, feeling like more of a football player than he ever had in his life.

Because he was as sore as he'd ever been in his life after all the hits he'd taken, including the one in particular that not only made him lose his breath, but made him think for a minute he'd never be able to find his breath again.

Yet here he was.

On the team.

A survivor.

"Now, boys, I want to make this crystal clear," Mr. Dolan said after they came out of the gym, where they'd changed out of their regular clothes and into the football gear. "Light contact means light contact tonight. I'm sure we're going to have the hardest hitters in the county on this team, but I don't need you trying to take a teammate's head off the very first night."

They did some basic blocking drills after that, divided up by weight like they were kids being assigned to different grades in school, even though everybody here was the same age. Scott knew from Chris that the weight limit was one hundred and fifty pounds in their league.

Great, Scott thought, *the big guys like Jimmy Dolan have me by fifty pounds.*

Mr. Dolan had been a star middle linebacker at Ohio State, something he'd told them when he introduced himself before the first practice on Monday night. It was almost like, "Hi, I'm Dick Dolan. I'm your coach, and I played for Ohio State."

Tonight he said that proper tackling was proper tackling no matter what level of football you played, sixth-grade ball or Pop Warner or college or the pros. So he showed them how he wanted them to set themselves and lower their shoulders and square themselves in front of the ballcarrier and drive right through him.

But that was for games, he said.

For tonight, he wanted them to get into solid position, but then just put their arms around the ballcarrier and hold up when he blew his whistle.

Scott was with the backs on both offense and defense, even though he kept tripping over his own feet when the coaches were showing how to back-pedal in order to cover a receiver. The second time he fell, he was so embarrassed that he reached down and started fussing with the laces on his high-top black shoes, as though they were untied.

Near the end of practice Mr. Dolan had them line up eleven against eleven and told them they were going to run some simple handoff plays with Chris at quarterback. Each back was to carry the ball one time and then switch over to defense, while somebody from defense would come over and get a carry.

There was nothing very tricky about it. Chris would take the ball from center, spin around—another thing he made look easy—and put the ball in somebody's stomach. Then that guy would try to gain a few yards before somebody wrapped him up and Mr. Dolan blew his whistle.

When it was finally Scott's turn, he wasn't thinking about even getting as far as the line of scrimmage.

He just wanted to put two hands on the ball and not drop it.

He didn't think he was going to get the ball from Chris and suddenly turn into LaDainian Tomlinson or Reggie Bush or Tiki Barber, break into the clear, run for the daylight that the TV announcers were always talking about.

Scott Parry was just praying that for once those small hands of his were going to hold on to the stupid ball.

By now, they all knew Chris would say "hut hut hut" and get the ball on the third "hut." The only thing the guys on defense didn't know was whether they were going to run right or left. They were supposed to read the way Chris turned and which way the blockers were going.

In the huddle, Chris told Scott they were running right this time.

Chris said, "No matter what happens, keep your legs moving, even after you hear the whistle."

"I can't *feel* my legs," Scott whispered to him.

The fullback got down into his stance in front of Scott. Scott was standing behind him, crouched over a little, hands on his thighs the way Mr. Dolan had showed him.

Please, he thought, *let this be just one time when I look as if I belong here.*

On the third "hut" he moved forward and to his

right, his hands in the position that the coaches had shown them for receiving the ball: Right arm underneath, palm up. Left arm on top, palm down. Chris spun to his right, put the ball in perfect position. Scott squeezed the ball between his arms, telling himself he wasn't letting go, no matter what.

Scott knew he was supposed to "read" the blocking ahead of him—that's the way Mr. Dolan had put it—and then either run inside or outside the right tackle.

He never made it that far.

Jimmy Dolan, playing middle linebacker like his dad had, blew right through the opening between the right guard and the right tackle before they even had the chance to straighten up and *try* to block him. Then, ignoring what his own dad had said about no tackling, he piled right into Scott, putting his helmet into Scott's stomach right below where the ball was.

Scott never had the chance to think about stepping left or right.

From the ground, the only direction he could see was up.

From what sounded like the other end of the field, Scott thought he heard a whistle blowing.

Or maybe that was just all the air in his body coming out of him at once.

The next thing he heard after the faraway sound of the whistle was Jimmy, still on top of him, saying, "Sorry, brain. Guess I got a little carried away."

Then Chris was there, yelling, "Get off of him, Jimmy!"

But Jimmy yelled right back, "Take a chill pill, Conlan! I just didn't hear the whistle in time to stop myself."

"Right," Chris said, pushing Jimmy out of the way.

"This *is* still tackle football, right?" Jimmy said.

"Yeah," Chris said. "And you're the tackling dummy."

Then Mr. Dolan was there with Chris, telling Scott to try to relax, he just got the wind knocked out of him. "Sit up if you can," he said. "But easy does it."

Chris put his hand behind Scott's back, gently

helped him up, took his helmet off, said, "Your face is pretty red. You okay yet?"

All Scott could do was shake his head.

He still couldn't breathe.

When he finally did get some air back into him, he suddenly started coughing so hard that Chris, not sure what to do, started patting him on the back, as if that would make him stop.

When he stopped coughing, Scott was at least able to make a joke out of it.

"Were you trying to burp me?" he said to Chris.

"Sorry."

Mr. Dolan said, "Put your head down for one more second, just to make sure."

Scott did. That's when he realized something.

He was still holding on to the ball.

SEVEN

The first official practice, for all the guys who had made it through the evaluations and still wanted to play sixth-grade football, was the next Saturday.

Scott did his own count, saw that nobody had dropped out after Wednesday. Still twenty-six survivors. After they'd finished, Mr. Dolan called them all together at midfield and told them that playing on his team was going to require almost as serious a commitment to hard work as school did.

"Hard work and hard hitting," he said.

There would be three night practices during the week, he said, and one on Saturday mornings until they started playing games on Saturday.

The six-game schedule would begin in two

weeks, one game against each of the other seven teams in their league.

Their team would be called the Eagles.

"I know that doesn't sound like a lot of games," Mr. Dolan said when practice was over. "But this is a small town, and we play in a small league." He was kneeling in front of the whole group, wearing a cap with an *O* on it that Scott knew was from Ohio State. "This is the first time for me coaching at this level, and I know it's the first time playing organized football for a lot of you guys. But we're still out here to win. All I've ever been about in football, going back to when I was your age, was winning, and that isn't going to change now. Starting today, I'm going to do whatever it takes to make this a winning team. Do you all understand that?"

Some of the guys nodded. Some mumbled, "Yeah."

Mr. Dolan suddenly turned into one of those drill sergeants you'd see in a movie, yelling, "I can't *hear* you. Is this going to be a winning team?"

"Yes!" they yelled back at him.

"See?" Mr. Dolan said. "You're learning already."

"Now there's one other thing you need to understand," he continued. "Now that the evaluations are over, the tryouts begin."

Scott looked around. Everybody else seemed as confused as he was. Everybody had made such a big deal out of calling the first three nights "evalations."

"What that means," Mr. Dolan said, "is that just because you have a uniform and a number doesn't guarantee you a spot out on that field. It doesn't work that way in our league. The only thing I can promise you is that if you're willing to learn, which means willing to be coached, then you're going to learn more about football in the next couple of months than you ever thought you could." He paused then and said, "And that's just in practice."

Mr. Dolan stood up, making a face as he did, then rubbing his right knee hard before he started talking again. Scott had already noticed that he limped a little when he moved around the field.

"I'll explain this all to your parents at our meeting," he said. "But this isn't one of those football leagues where everybody has to play a certain amount of downs. Playing time is up to me and my coaches. If we don't think you're ready to play tackle football, even at this level, then practice players is all some of you are going to be this season."

Scott had one knee on the ground, his right hand resting on his helmet, trying to look like Chris and Jimmy.

Mr. Dolan was standing right over him now.

In Scott's mind, the coach wasn't talking to the whole team.

He was speaking directly to him.

"What you're really going to find out this season is just how much you love football," he said.

Scott wanted to say, Don't worry, Coach, I already know.

If I didn't love it, I wouldn't still be here.

The only time he had gotten to scrimmage today was at the very end, when Mr. Dolan put him in on the kickoff team.

Nick Donegan, the only kid on the team bigger than Jimmy Dolan, was kicking the ball off. Jeremy

Sharp, the fastest kid on their team, was back by himself receiving. Scott was on the far left, as close to the sideline as they could put him, hoping he could run down the field and get somewhere near Jeremy Sharp without falling all over himself.

No chance.

He made it about three steps before he tripped over his own feet again. By the time he picked himself up, Jeremy had grabbed Nick's line-drive kick on one bounce, dodged the first couple of tacklers, made Nick miss, made Jimmy Dolan miss, cut to his right, broke into the clear down the sideline.

Just one guy left to beat now:

Scott.

Who was feeling like he was out in the street and had a speeding car coming right for him.

He tried to stay calm, hard as his heart was beating, and squared himself up the way the coaches had shown them, reminded himself to be up on the balls of his feet in case Jeremy made another cut, this one back toward the middle of the field.

Jeremy didn't cut back.

Didn't have to.

He just switched the ball to his left hand and straight-armed Scott with his right, sending him flying out of bounds, making it look as if Scott was the one who had gotten tackled as Jeremy ran the rest of the way to the end zone.

"Hey, brain," Jimmy yelled from the middle of the field, even though all he'd tackled on the play was air, "at least you got your uniform dirty."

Yeah, he loved football, all right.

Scott didn't need a missed tackle to tell him he wasn't even close to being good. All he had to do was watch everybody else play eleven-on-eleven. You didn't have to ask if they loved football, or why they did. It was right there in front of your eyes. You saw it with Jimmy Dolan, as soon as he got out there and was allowed to start hitting people. You saw it with Jeremy Sharp, who looked like he was born to run the way he had down the sideline.

Most of all, you saw it with Chris Conlan.

This wasn't Parry Field. This wasn't anything like the Chris from Parry Field when he was playing catch with Scott, the one who was as much a cheerleader as a quarterback.

No, this was a whole different Chris Conlan, moving guys around on offense if they weren't lined up in the right place, running down the field and showing somebody like Jeremy that he'd run the wrong pass pattern, slapping the sides of his helmet with both hands when he was the one who'd made a mistake.

And as good as he was, he would make mistakes, like everybody else. Sometimes it was almost as if he was making them on purpose. Mr. Dolan would come into the huddle and bring a piece of paper with the Xs and Os on it, and then they'd get up to the line of scrimmage and the blockers would run one way and Chris would run the other.

Maybe he just doesn't want to look perfect every single second he's out there, Scott thought, *like he's so far above everybody else.*

But most of the time he was, not just looking better but looking older somehow, especially when Mr. Dolan would let him cut loose and throw a pass down the field. Or when he'd let Chris roll out and run with the ball himself. Chris would fight for every last yard, even when somebody managed to bring him down in the open field.

Scott didn't mind watching from the sidelines.

Just being there, just being on the team, getting to wear a uniform, that's what mattered.

He knew he'd probably never leave the sidelines and do something to belong with these guys. And that was okay.

It was still football.

Early Saturday afternoon.

Scott and Chris were lying in grass that had just been cut the day before, that cool, cut-grass smell all around them, a summer smell, watching the dogs chase each other around the goalposts, the sun warm enough on their faces that they really could still pretend it was summer vacation.

Scott had been doing most of the talking, but only because Chris hadn't been doing any talking at all since practice had ended. He'd tried to act like he was in a good mood in front of Scott's mom when they were back at the house having lunch, but now he was like the complete opposite, as though he was barely listening.

Like he wished he wasn't there.

Scott decided to ask him a question he'd been wanting to ask anyway. Just came right out with it.

"How come you wanted to be friends with me?" he said, not looking at Chris, just staring straight up at the sky. Hoping Chris wouldn't laugh at him. Or say something like "Who said anything about being friends?"

Or get weirded out and just get up and leave.

He didn't do any of those things.

"Dogs," he said.

"Dogs?"

Chris rolled over, propping himself up on an elbow. "No lie," he said. "It started when I saw you had that picture of Casey that day."

"Aw, man, that is *so* not cool."

"It was to me," Chris said. "'Cause it's the way I feel about Brett, even though I'd never tell any of the guys that."

"So we're hanging out because we both like dogs?"

"I'm not good at talking about myself," Chris said.

Scott grinned. "My mom says guys never are."

Chris rolled back over, like maybe he could find the right words in the sky. "When you talk about how hard you try, I could see that even before I knew you," Chris said. "Does that make any sense? *My* mom says that the best thing anybody can have going for them is heart. And, I don't know, somehow I could see you had heart even before we got out here."

He blew out some breath like even talking this much had made him tired.

For a long time, nobody said anything.

Then Chris said, "Can I ask you a question?"

"Yeah."

"How come you didn't tell Mr. D you could kick when he was looking for guys to kick off?"

"Are you joking? Did you see how fast Big Nick went for that tee?"

"You can kick, dude," Chris said. "But Coach'll never know that if you don't tell him."

"I can kick here," Scott said. "I can kick with only you and Casey watching. And you have to promise me you're not going to tell anybody."

"Why?" Chris said.

"Because I'm asking you to."

"I'm not promising until you tell me why," Chris said.

"Because I'm afraid, that's why," Scott said. He took a deep breath, wanting Chris to understand. "Because kicking is all I've got, and if I screw up, then I won't even have that anymore. I won't even be any good in my dreams."

"For a guy I said had heart, you can sound like such a baby sometimes!" Chris said.

It came at Scott loud—and out of nowhere, like a clap of thunder you didn't know was coming. Like something had been building up inside him since they'd gotten out here and now he had just popped.

"What . . . ?" was all Scott could get out.

Chris Conlan wasn't through.

He was on his feet, on fire.

"You want to be afraid about something?" Chris was really yelling now. "How about somebody taking your whole stinking season away?"

Then he picked up the ball and threw it as far as Scott had ever seen him throw it, toward the woods. Casey went running after it at top speed from all the way at the other end of the field, barking his head off, Brett trailing way behind, making the squeaky noise that passed for his own bark.

"Dude," Scott said, when he thought it was safe to say anything, "what does that mean, somebody's going to take your season away?"

Chris turned toward the water now. Scott couldn't get a good look at his face and wasn't sure he wanted to, because the coolest kid in school was blinking his eyes, fast, biting down on his lower lip, like he might start crying any second.

"I've been wanting to tell you for a couple of days," Chris said finally. "I might have to quit the team before the season even starts."

"Quit the team?" Scott said. "You can't quit the team. You're the best player. There *is* no team without you."

"Doesn't matter."

"Why?"

"Because I can't read," Chris said.

Then he turned and ran.

EIGHT

Scott was afraid to call Chris the rest of Saturday.

He wanted to call him, wanted in the worst way to understand what was going on with the only friend he had at school.

But he didn't pick up the phone. He thought about going online and trying to instant-message him, which sometimes was an easier way to talk to somebody.

He didn't do that, either.

He mostly just sat up in his room, Casey lying there on the floor next to his bed, thinking the same thing over and over again: How crazy this was.

This was Chris Conlan. How could he be this crazy about some book he was having trouble reading?

Except that's not the way it came out. It came out like he couldn't read at all. But how could that be? Everybody could read by the time they got to the sixth grade.

Couldn't they?

When he finally left his room for dinner that night, his mom said, "Did you and Chris have some sort of fight?"

"No."

He stared at his plate like he was trying to read something.

"Because he left in a pretty big hurry."

"There was no fight, Mom."

No way he was going to tell his parents what had happened. Chris hadn't said it was a secret, hadn't said another word before he'd bolted. But Scott wasn't taking any chances until he talked to him again.

Still his mom, being a mom, wouldn't let it go.

She said, "He just came in, asked if he could use the phone to call his mom, then said he was going to wait outside for her. Then when you didn't come back right away—"

"Mom!" It came out too loud and Scott knew it. "Nothing happened!"

"Don't raise your voice to your mother, bud," his dad said. "She didn't do anything."

"Sorry," he said.

He wanted to ask his parents if there was any way somebody as smart as Chris couldn't read. Or if it was possible that any sixth-grader couldn't read.

But he had made up his mind that he wasn't going to say anything to anybody until he saw Chris at school on Monday.

He didn't have to wait that long.

Every Sunday Scott and his parents had brunch at their favorite restaurant in town, the New Paradise Café.

They would leave their car at church and walk down Main Street and usually sit in the first room at the New Paradise. Scott ordered the same thing every time: blueberry pancakes, tall stack.

Today Scott had polished off his stack in record time, finished eating so fast that his parents weren't even close to finishing their omelets. He asked them if he could walk down to the video store, which opened at noon on Sundays, then meet them back here in a little while.

His dad gave him some money, saying, "In honor of making the team, you can rent a game if you want."

"Dad," Scott said, "I didn't make anything, and you know it. I just stuck it out."

"So get a game in honor of that," his dad said.

"I'm not any better at football this week than I was last week."

"You know what we say in this family," his dad said, smiling that smile at him. "You don't always get to pick the things you're best at."

Scott was walking toward Gramophone Video, still thinking about Chris because he hadn't been thinking about anything else since yesterday, when he saw Chris walking toward him, along with Jimmy Dolan and Jeremy Sharp.

No place to hide.

He wanted to see Chris, but not like this. Certainly not with Jimmy Dolan in the picture.

"Hey, look, it's the brain," Jimmy said. "All duded up."

They were all stopped now, in front of Thayer's Hardware.

"Hey, guys," Scott said, trying to ignore Jimmy as usual.

"Hey," Jeremy said.

Chris didn't say anything, just kicked some invisible pebble on the sidewalk. Scott couldn't believe Chris would be hanging out with Jimmy. Maybe he'd just run into the other guys at the video store.

Scott said to Chris, "I was going to give you a shout-out later."

Jimmy said, "You been hanging out with the brain, Conlan? What for—you need help with your homework?"

Scott thought, *Of all the things in the whole world this dope could have said, he had to say that.*

Chris looked over Scott's head, down Main Street, and said, "I don't need any help from the brain to do my homework."

Scott felt as if all the air had gone out of him, like a ball with a hole in it.

Before anybody else could say anything, Chris said, "I gotta go. My mom's picking me up in front of Lou's."

A diner at the other end of Main.

"We'll go with you," Jimmy Dolan said. "See you around, brain."

He laughed then, as if he'd cracked himself up.

Scott stayed right where he was, didn't turn to watch them go, didn't care about the sound of Jimmy's laughter, which to Scott was always the same as a fingernail being scratched across a blackboard.

The only thing he could really hear—still—was Chris calling him "the brain."

He didn't turn around until he was sure they were gone. Then he walked slowly back to the New Paradise Café, hoping his parents were ready to go home.

Because he was.

Casey was waiting for him, the way he always was.

He was waiting right behind the front door, spinning around in excitement, acting as if Scott had been away forever.

At least Casey never let him down.

Scott ran upstairs, changed into his play clothes as fast as he could, grabbed his football. When Casey saw the ball, he immediately ran through the kitchen and to the back door, barking all over again, kept barking all the way through the woods until they were back out on Parry Field.

It seemed like more than just a day since Scott and Chris had been out here.

More than that, it seemed to Scott that he was right back where he started.

Him and Case.

Alone.

He should have known it wasn't going to last with Chris Conlan, no matter what Chris had said about them having dogs in common. No matter what he'd said about Scott having heart.

When Scott got close enough to the goalposts, he fired a pass as hard as he could at the tire.

Missed by a mile.

Casey didn't care. He chased after the ball like this was their regular game on a regular day, as if nothing had changed, even though Scott felt as if everything had changed.

Even if he couldn't figure out why.

Chris had acted in town as if Scott was the one who had done something, when all Scott had done the day before was listen. How was listening somebody's fault?

In town it was like he and Chris hardly knew each other, as if it had been somebody else who stuck up for him with Jimmy Dolan at the bus that day, somebody else pushing Scott to go out for football and then hang in there, no matter what, so he could make a team for the first time in his life.

Now it was a team he didn't even want to be on anymore.

He was better off here.

Scott kept throwing the ball, managed eventually to put a couple through the tire, Casey always bringing the ball back for another try. Then it was time for Scott to start kicking, first off the tee, then some dropkicks.

For some reason, even though that big heart Chris had talked about wasn't really in it, he couldn't miss with his dropkicks today.

He was on fire.

He hardly ever made a lot of dropkicks in a row, mostly because all you had to do was be a little off dropping the ball to throw everything off.

You could miss your spot. Or the ball would land crooked. Stuff like that.

Today he had made six in a row.

He wasn't just money today. He was *cash*. That's what his dad would say when they were out here together and Scott would really nail one. In fact, his dad was supposed to be out here by now, he'd said that he was coming out for one of their Sunday kicking contests for the championship of the entire known universe as soon as he made a couple of quick Sunday business calls.

But Scott wasn't waiting for him now as he went for seven in a row, which would have been his all-time record. He was in the zone. Could not miss.

He made number seven.

Casey started barking, as if somehow he knew that Scott had earned a cheer, then went after the ball.

But instead of bringing the ball right back, Casey suddenly ran in the opposite direction, back toward the woods.

"Case, get back here," Scott called out, his voice so loud on the empty field it sounded like it was coming out of speakers on a real field.

No sound from Casey.

No sight of his crazy dog.

Didn't he know that when you got hot like this, when you had this kind of rhythm going for you, you didn't want to wait? You wanted to kick the next one right away.

Only now his dog was freezing the kicker the way the other team did sometimes in the pros by calling a time-out.

"Case!" Scott yelled. "This is *definitely* delay of game."

He started to go after him, then saw Casey coming out of the woods.

Only he didn't have the ball with him.

Just Brett.

Chris was right behind them.

He had the ball now.

"I think this belongs to you," he said.

NINE

"I came to say I'm sorry," Chris said.

"It's cool."

"No, it's not cool," he said. "I was out of line. Like way out of line. Calling you the brain like Jimmy does." He shook his head. "Talking to you like that . . . that's not me."

"I thought maybe I did something," Scott said.

"Not you. Me. I'm the stupid one."

"Not a problem."

They were sitting in the grass. The dogs were gone.

Chris said, "I'm the one with the problem."

"When you're friends with somebody," Scott said, "then it's your problem, too." He stopped there for a second, not wanting this to come out sounding like some big deal. But knowing that it was, right now, the biggest possible deal. "And you and me . . . we're still friends, right?"

"We're friends," Chris said, "even if I didn't act like one in town."

"Now all you've gotta do is tell me what the problem is," Scott said. "Reading or being on the team?"

"Both."

Then he tried to explain to Scott about dyslexia.

And how it could drag him down from behind better than any tackler on a football field.

"You ever get cramps?" Chris said.

"Don't laugh," Scott said, "but I get them in my feet sometimes."

"What I've got," Chris said, "is like a permanent cramp of my brain."

He said that he and Scott would read the same page in a book, but that some of the words would sound different inside his brain than Scott's.

He said he could look at a word like *pen* and

read *pin* instead, and then get confused, not knowing why somebody in the book was trying to write with a pin.

Or, Chris said, he'd read a word at the top of a page and then forget what it meant by the time he got down to the bottom.

Writing, he said, was even worse.

"I'm okay if I have to get up in class and talk about something we had to read, as long as I worked really, really hard on it the night before with my mom or one of my tutors," he said. "But when I try to write out the same answer, I'll just be getting started when you guys are putting your notebooks away."

All of a sudden, Scott felt like he'd been in a dark room and somebody had hit the light switch.

"It's why you run the wrong way sometimes," he said, "on the field."

Chris reached over and bumped him some fist. "If Mr. Dolan shows me the Xs and Os on a page, I get crossed up sometimes, just the way I do with my reading. But if he tells me what to do, then I'm pretty much good to go. It's why even on some of our simplest plays sometimes, I ask him to break down every part of it, even have him walk through it like he's the quarterback. That way I can really see it."

But football wasn't his problem, he said, even if he was the only one running right sometimes when the rest of the team was running left.

School was the problem, and it was getting worse, even though the year had just started.

"How are you when you have to work on the computer and type stuff?" Scott said.

"I'm the king of IM-ing people," he said, "because nobody cares if you're a lousy speller or not."

"I still don't get how this means you might have to quit the team," Scott said.

Chris took a deep breath, let it out in a long whoosh. "Here's the deal," he said. "If I can't keep up this year, they want to put me in Special Ed. And I'm already not keeping up."

Scott felt like the slow one now. "But what does this have to do with football?"

Chris said his parents had laid it out for him

like this: If he couldn't show that he was keeping up in his classes by the time the season started in a couple of weeks, then they were going to hire a full-time tutor. Full-time meant four nights a week. The tutor's job was to get him ready for this big state equivalency test at the end of the semester.

"If I can pass that, I can stay in our regular class," he said. "If I can't, I go into Special Ed."

"And that's a bad thing?"

"Listen, every grown-up who talks to me says that Special Ed isn't like school for dummies," he said. "They say that sometimes the opposite is true, that some of the smartest kids end up in Special Ed for all kinds of different reasons, not just dyslexia. But I don't care. I want to stay with my friends."

"Dude," Scott said, "nobody's gonna think any differently about you whatever class you're in. You're . . . you're *you.*"

"You hear what the other kids say about Special Ed kids."

"Well, then, you can be the one to show those kids that they're the ones acting dumber than dirt."

Chris's face started to get red.

His eyes, too.

"I just want things to stay the way they are," he said. "I want to be with my regular teachers. I want to be with my friends. And I want to keep playing football instead of getting tutored every stinking night."

"Your parents wouldn't really make you quit the team," Scott said, "would they?"

"Two weeks," Chris said. "I've got two weeks."

"Then we need a plan."

"Yeah, and here it is: In the next two weeks I've got to become more like you."

Scott couldn't help it when he heard that.

He laughed.

"You think this is funny?"

No, Scott said, it wasn't that at all.

"It's just that nobody ever said that to me before," he said.

Scott didn't have a plan. He didn't have anything close to a plan. He sat there feeling as helpless as he did at sports sometimes.

It was Chris who changed the subject, just by standing up, grabbing the ball, motioning for Scott to get up and go long.

Scott did that, running away from the goalposts at Parry Field, running down the sideline until he couldn't see the white line underneath his sneakers anymore.

When he looked back, the ball was right on top of him.

Unfortunately, so were the dogs.

They had come running back out of the woods at the worst possible moment, Casey in the lead, tracking the ball as if Chris was throwing it to him instead of to Scott, cutting Scott off the way a free safety would, and taking his legs right out from under him.

The ball landed harmlessly in the grass.

"My own dog can cover me," Scott said to himself.

Even Casey's better at football than I am.

And then, for some weird reason, it wasn't his own voice inside his head, it was his dad's.

From brunch.

You don't always get to pick the things you're best at.

Sitting there, brand-new grass stains all over his knees, the idea came to him. And not just any old idea. A totally fantastically brilliant idea.

He jumped up and tried to beat Casey back to where Chris was standing at the other end of the field.

Out of breath he said to Chris, "Make you a deal."

"Deal," Chris said, "or no deal."

Trying to sound like the guy on the TV show.

"No, really," Scott said. "Listen to me. The deal is, you make me better at football, and I'll make you better at school."

Scott was feeling *so* brilliant.

"And how are you going to do that, exactly?" Chris said.

"You forget something," Scott said, almost in a cocky way.

"What's that?"

"I'm the brain."

It was later that same afternoon, and Scott and Chris were in the Conlans' living room with Chris's mom and dad.

"Nothing else we've tried has worked out that great," Chris said. "Why can't we try this?"

Scott and Chris had done most of the talking from the time they'd all sat down, taking turns like they were some kind of tag team, not really giving Chris's parents a chance to interrupt them. That was always the way you did it with your parents when you weren't just talking to them, but trying to talk them into something.

When you were afraid that the second you stopped talking they were going to say no.

Only that didn't happen, at least not right away.

All Chris's dad said, in a nice way, was, "Are you two finished?"

Chris's dad was tall, the way Chris was, and looked like an athlete. But Chris said he really wasn't, that all he did was jog. He had no real interest in sports unless he was watching one of Chris's games.

"You two really think you can pull this off?" Bill Conlan said.

"We do," Scott and Chris said, almost at the exact same time.

"I've heard what a wonderful student you are," Chris's dad said to Scott now.

"Not as good as he says I am."

"I doubt that, just listening to you speak today, the way you present things. But you're talking about being the first eleven-year-old teaching assistant I believe I've ever heard of."

Chris's mom hadn't said anything yet. She was mostly smiling, like she knew something the rest of them didn't.

"All we're asking for is a shot," Chris said.

"For two weeks," Scott said.

"Scott," Chris's dad said, "has Chris really explained to you the issues he has in the classroom?"

"Yes."

"And you're saying you can help him get past them?"

"No, that's not what I'm saying." Then he added, "Sir."

"No?"

"I'm saying that I'm willing to try, Mr. Conlan," he said. "And my mom says she's willing to help, too. She used to be a guidance counselor before she married my dad, and she says she can help me plan stuff out." He turned toward Chris, grinning. "Like a game plan."

"I'd rather have Scott than another new tutor," Chris said.

Now Mrs. Conlan said, "Maybe this is so crazy it might work, Bill. Peer support instead of peer pressure."

"It's going to work!" Chris said. "I'm going to work twice as hard as I ever have!"

"Your plan is to study before every practice, is that right?" Bill Conlan said.

"That's the plan," Scott said. "Sometimes here, sometimes at my house."

"And you study together from then until it's time for football?"

Scott and Chris nodded, hard.

Mrs. Conlan, whose first name was Gail, said, "And two weeks from today, we talk to Chris's teachers and see where he is."

Talking about it like it was a done deal already.

Scott and Chris waited, not saying anything now.

Then Chris's dad looked at his mom, turned back to them and said, "You've got a deal."

"Yessssss!" Chris said, leaning over in his chair to bump fists with Scott and nearly falling over as he did.

Then the two of them were running out of the living room, colliding with each other in the Con-lans' front hall before heading up the stairs to Chris's room.

When the door was closed, Chris said, "Do you really think we can pull this off?"

"I do if you do," Scott said. "Who's the one always saying that you can't do stuff in sports unless you think you can?"

"I am *so* hearing you," Chris said.

Then Scott told Chris to get out the flash cards he said he tried to use for English sometimes, so the two of them could get busy.

It wasn't so long ago that Scott was the new kid at school.

Now he was the new teacher.

ELEVEN

After the first week of real practice, with one more week to go until the first game, Scott's dad said to him one night at dinner, "So what position do you think you're going to end up playing?"

Being serious.

Scott decided not to paint one of those dopey smiley faces on the whole thing.

"I don't have a position," he said, trying to make himself look busy cutting another piece of steak. "I'm probably not going to have one, either, other than maybe glorified water boy."

"Oh, come on, it's still way too early to be talking like that."

"Dad, we play our first game in a week."

Hank Parry said, "Most coaches I ever had

wanted to keep guys off balance about who was going to get the most playing time until the last possible moment."

So his dad was the one drawing the smiley face.

As usual.

"Well, he must love me, Dad. Because I'm *always* off balance."

His dad laughed and said, "Good one, kiddo."

Yeah, Scott thought, *when it comes to football, I'm hilarious.*

"Well, does he have you working more on offense or defense?" his dad said.

"Special teams."

It was the truth. Not that it made him feel very special. When he did get on the field now, it was almost always as one of the guys running downfield on punts, even if he hadn't made a single tackle yet. Not one. He'd be close to the guy with the ball sometimes, even throw himself down near the real tacklers just to feel as if he'd been part of the play. But he knew he wasn't fooling anybody.

Starting with himself.

Sometimes on punts Mr. Dolan would put him on the receiving team, on the outside, lining him up against the fast guys who could actually run down and make a tackle, telling him to try to throw a block as a way of slowing them down.

Then another outside guy on the kick team would run around him as if he wasn't even there.

Jimmy Dolan, just for the fun of it, would go out of his way to knock Scott down before running down the field, even though he knew it would cost him a few seconds getting to the punt returner, and that he would hear it from his dad when the play was over. Which he did.

"Use your head once in a while," Mr. Dolan would say to Jimmy, trying to act as hard on him as he was on everybody else, even though not one single player on the team believed it. They knew that Jimmy got away with stuff that nobody else on the team could, stuff nobody would even dream about *trying* to get away with on the field.

"Sorry, brain," Jimmy would say when the play was over. "But there's just something about putting you on the ground that is so totally awesome. It's like I'm racking up points playing video."

Water boy would actually be a step up, he realized.

"Your chance will come," his dad said from across the dinner table now.

"Dad, I'm trying not to get my hopes up," Scott said. "All I see myself doing this year is riding the bench, unless we're winning, like, 100–0."

His dad put down his knife and fork and in a soft voice said to him, "Hey, what happened to my Rudy?"

Rudy was one of their favorite sports movies to watch together. No, that wasn't right. It was one of their favorite movies, period. The story of the Notre Dame guy, a little guy who wasn't supposed to make the team and then, once he was on the team, wasn't ever supposed to get in a game. But he finally got in for one play and made a tackle and got carried off the field by his teammates at the end.

It said on the screen at the end of the movie that it was the only time in the whole history of Notre

Dame football that any player had ever been carried off the field.

"You just gotta be ready for your Rudy moment," his dad said.

"But what difference does it make if I'm ready if I can't even make a tackle in practice?" Scott said. "If the only person I can bring down most of the time is myself?"

"Yet," his dad said. "You haven't made a tackle *yet.*"

Scott said, "The only big play I'm gonna make this season is in your dreams."

"Let me worry about my dreams," his dad said. "You just worry about your own."

He called into the den and told his parents he was going to take Casey for a walk.

"With the leash," his dad said.

"Case won't go anywhere," Scott said.

"Case goes everywhere," his dad called back, "especially at night. And, besides, you know the rules."

"At night he's on the leash."

"And don't—"

"—leave the neighborhood."

Casey had never liked being on a leash, from the time he was a pup. But he knew the leash was a signal he was going outside, and he loved going outside. So he'd get almost as excited when he saw Scott with the leash in his hands as he did when Scott came walking down stairs with a ball.

"Let's go, pal," Scott said.

Casey's answer was to come sliding right into Scott on their slippery kitchen floor.

As soon as they were out the door, Casey was pulling him down the front walk. It was completely dark by now, and the old-fashioned streetlights were lit. When they got to the sidewalk, Scott saw a woman he recognized from up the block walking at them from the other direction, power-walking the way his mom did sometimes, earphones in her ears.

As she passed them, she said to Scott, "Very cool dog."

Scott smiled and said, "I know," wondering if she even heard him over whatever it was she was listening to.

When the sound of her footsteps was gone, there was just the panting Casey the dog, straining against the leash the way he always did once they got going, wanting Scott to go faster.

Alone on the street, Scott began to announce an imaginary game.

"Welcome to Bloomfield North Field," he said. "It's a perfect morning for football as the Eagles prepare to open their season against their cross-town rival, the Jets."

Not a great voice, he thought.

But not bad.

"The Eagles have won the toss and elected to receive," he said.

On the quiet street, his voice sounding loud, Scott said, "Scott Parry to kick off. . . ."

Chris's big day in class was the Thursday before their first game.

Mr. Dykes, their English teacher, was going to give them a passage from a book, ask them to read it in an allotted period of time, then quiz them on it right after they finished reading.

Quiz them and grade them.

"It will be like a homework assignment, just in class," Mr. Dykes had told them on Monday. "And it will give me a good read, early in the semester, on your ability to not just read, but understand what you're reading."

On the bus home on Monday, Chris had said, "If I have to read a chapter fast, I'm done like dinner. You know how slow I read."

"So you pick up a step by Thursday," Scott had said.

"You sound pretty confident."

"I am."

Actually, he wasn't.

That afternoon they figured out that it took Chris about two minutes to read a page. The book they were using was one they were reading in school, called *My Brother Sam Is Dead,* about a family during the Revolutionary War.

When Scott put himself on the clock, they found out he needed fifty-five seconds to read the same page.

"Great," Chris said. "You're more than twice as fast as me."

Scott smiled.

Chris said, "You're smiling *because*?"

"Because I just came up with another one of my brilliant ideas."

"Your brilliant ideas usually mean more work for me," Chris said.

"You want to hear it or not?"

"Do I have a choice?"

"Nah."

"Before we get to Mr. Dykes's class on Friday," he said, "your time is going *down,* sucker."

"You sound like Mr. Dolan when he takes his stopwatch out."

"Exactly," Scott said. "You're going to compete. Against yourself. And I'm going to time you."

The hero of *My Brother Sam Is Dead* was a boy named Tim Meeker, and the story was about how his brother Sam runs off to fight for the American rebels and against the British army in the late 1770s, before America won its independence. Scott, who'd finished the whole book even though the class hadn't been required to do that yet, thought it was a solid book. Chris was only about halfway through, but Scott could see that he was getting into it, too.

"I still can't believe I actually like a book," Chris said.

Scott looked at him, curious now. "You've never read just for the fun of it?"

Chris shook his head. "Would you, if you were me? And who said this is fun, anyway?"

"You're liking this book, you said so yourself."

"I like it okay."

"That's good enough for now," Scott said.

As the week went on, Scott saw the athlete in Chris coming out a little more every day, saw how competitive he was getting, how he was pushing himself. Could see how Chris would finish a page, say "done," then look at Scott and ask with his eyes what his time was without saying a word.

"Eighty-five seconds," Scott would say.

Or eighty-three. Whatever it was. Chris seemed to knock off a couple of seconds every time Scott put him on the clock.

When they did their last page on Wednesday, studying at Scott's this time, he got under eighty seconds for the first time.

"And I slowed down for a second when I got here," Chris said, pointing to the word *sight*. "Another one that doesn't sound the way it looks," he said.

Words like that, ones he couldn't sound out, were still a problem for him, Scott had discovered. But he kept telling Chris that he couldn't let words like that make him feel like he'd run into a door.

"You just gotta keep moving," Scott said.

Chris grinned. "Like I'm getting chased by a couple of linebackers."

"If you stop," Scott said, "you're gonna get sacked."

"Mr. Dolan calls it getting dough-popped," Chris said. "Some kind of Southern expression."

"Yeah," Scott said. "And, remember, *dough* is spelled d-o-u-g-h."

"I hate words like that!"

Scott said, "Get over it and start reading the next page." Pointing to his watch as he said that.

"You have turned into Mr. Dolan," Chris said.

They read until Scott's mom said Chris's mom was there to pick him up. Wednesday wasn't a practice night this week, but they were studying together anyway, because the test was tomorrow.

When Chris was gone, Scott's mom said, "So how are we looking there, Professor?"

"Chris calls me Coach."

"So how is he doing, really? He seems to be in a much better mood lately. Mrs. Conlan says she's noticed it, too."

Scott said, "He's gotten a lot better in just a week. The last page we did today, he had his best time ever. Then I had him read a whole chapter and talk about it afterward. Mom," Scott said, excited, "he *got* it."

"You think he can get through this tomorrow?"

"He's definitely nervous," Scott said. "Chris said he never chokes at football, but when it comes to quizzes, he gags his lungs out."

"You're more nervous about his test than you've ever been for one of your own."

"Not even close," Scott said.

She put her arms around him then. "Have I told you lately what a great kid you are?"

Scott said, "Well, not in months and months."

"You are an unbelievably great kid."

"Thanks, Mom."

"You are most welcome."

Scott looked up at his mom and said, "He's got to nail this sucker."

THIRTEEN

Chris nailed it.

They didn't know for sure he'd nailed it that day, because they weren't getting their grades until the next morning. At lunch all Chris said was that he thought he'd done a solid job.

"I was going to stop a couple of times," he said. "I'd get stuck on a word and get that bad feeling. But I made myself keep going, like we talked about."

English, their last class before lunch, had just ended a few minutes before, and he was still all fired up, like he really had just played a big game. "The whole time, I pictured you standing over me, looking at that cheesy watch of yours."

Scott said, "What do you mean, cheesy? Do

you know how many tickets at the video arcade this watch cost me?"

The book Mr. Dykes had given them was called *Hoot*, about some cool kids in Florida trying to save baby owls. He'd had them read the first chapter, then told them to write an essay about what had happened and how they felt the author had made them want to read the rest of the book.

When Mr. Dykes handed them back their blue books on Friday, Scott could feel himself holding his breath the way he would during the best parts of a movie, could actually feel his heart beating inside his chest.

Chris stared at the grade on the front, not changing expression until Mr. Dykes was past him, then holding up the front of the book so that Scott could see the grade written in red Magic Marker on the front:

B.

Scott knew that the best Chris had done on the first three quizzes so far this semester was a C-minus.

Making sure Mr. Z couldn't see, Chris pointed across at Scott and mouthed "you."

Scott smiled, then shook his head.

When Mr. Dykes dropped the blue book on his desk, Scott saw the A at the top and "Excellent work!" underneath that.

He felt much better about the B across the room.

That night, after talking to Mr. Dykes on the telephone, Mr. and Mrs. Conlan made it official that Chris could stay on the team. The next day Chris scored two touchdowns as the Eagles beat the Jets, 12–6.

Scott didn't play a single down, just watched from the sidelines, helmet on his head the whole time, standing about twenty yards from Mr. Dolan, trying not to cheer for Chris every single time he made a good play, because that made him feel more like a cheerleader than a teammate.

When the game was over, Chris ran straight for Scott, so he could bump him some fist.

"First the quiz, now the game," Scott said. "You're on a roll, dude."

Chris shook his head slowly from side to side. "*We're* on a roll," he said. "You and me, we're a team now."

In the classroom, Scott wanted to say to him.

In the classroom we're a team.

Never on the field.

They won the next Saturday, against the Bears, and then the Saturday after that, against the Rams, to make it 3–0 for the season.

Chris was great against the Bears, even throwing a touchdown pass to Jimmy Dolan. But it was Grant Dillon, their fullback, a guy usually only in there to block in the backfield for Chris or Jeremy Sharp, who saved them against the Rams. Jeremy had rolled his ankle early in the fourth quarter and had to sit out the rest of the game. After that, Chris was the one running with the ball—when he wasn't trying an occasional pass, even though Mr. Dolan liked passing about as much as he liked referees.

The Rams were ahead, 6–0.

By the time the Eagles got the ball with two

minutes left, the Ram defenders had figured out that if they sent everybody after Chris on every play and double-covered Jimmy when he went out for a pass, they were going to win the game.

But on third-and-four from the Eagles' forty-yard line, Chris crossed them up.

Big-time.

He took the snap and started rolling to his right. If you had been watching the game, it looked like every sweep he had been running to that side all day. Suddenly, though, he stopped, turned and threw the ball back across the field to Grant, who was wide open on the left sideline, nothing but green grass stretched out ahead of him.

Grant wasn't the fastest guy on their team. In fact, next to Scott, he was probably the slowest. But with most of the Rams chasing Chris, and Jimmy Dolan having taken his two defenders deep down the right side, he was in the clear.

The only two Rams with a chance were the ones down the field with Jimmy. But Jimmy blocked one of the guys somehow. Like he was a streak of light,

Chris appeared out of nowhere, thirty yards from the spot where he'd released the ball, to take down the other.

Grant ended up running sixty yards for the touchdown that made it 6–6, and Chris threw a pass to Jimmy for the conversion. The Eagles had won again.

When Mr. Dolan gathered the team around him at midfield after the game, he said, "*This* game is the one I've been talking about since the start of practice." He tapped the top of Grant's helmet lightly with his knuckle, like he was knocking on a door. "And this guy right here is the player I've been saying I want you all to be. When it was his turn to make a play, he was ready."

Mr. Dolan stood up then, putting his big right hand out in front of him, meaning it was time for the players to bring it in.

"I want the rest of you to go home today and think about the play Grant made for us and the game he won for us," Mr. Dolan said. "And tell yourself that you're going to be ready when your number's called."

Every number except mine, Scott thought as he put his hand in there with all the rest.

In the car on the way home, Scott's dad said, "I'm thinking about having a talk with your coach."

Scott was still in his uniform, helmet on his lap. "Dad, no."

"You don't even know what I want to talk to him about," his dad said.

"Yeah, I do. You want to get him to play me. But you always said you were never going to be one of those dads."

"And I'm not going to be one now. I'd just sort of like him to explain why he *won't* play you."

"Not just me," Scott said. "Eric Dodds, also. And Nik Solo."

"There's three of you? Good, then I'm not just talking about my own kid."

"We're not playing because we're not good enough," Scott said.

"To do what? Make it to the Pro Bowl this season?" Dialing up his voice just a little.

"Dad, you don't see our practices."

"I've seen enough to get a pretty good handle on things."

"If you saw us every day," Scott said, "I'm pretty sure you'd see what Mr. Dolan sees. Which is that I stink."

"You put in the time," his dad said. "You go to every practice. It seems to me he could reward you with a couple of downs here and there."

"He says he doesn't coach that way," Scott said. "He says it doesn't teach us anything about sports and it doesn't teach us anything about the real world."

"Which I'm sure he is a *huge* expert on," Hank Parry said. "He must have learned it all at the Ohio State–Michigan game."

They were in a line of traffic, waiting as a train went through town. Scott turned so his dad could see him smiling, not wanting him to make a big deal out of this. "This isn't like school," he said. "Coach isn't going to give me a gold star for perfect attendance."

"You're aware that you've already played half the season, right?"

"I can still do math," Scott said.

"You should get into a game."

"Dad, listen," Scott said when the car was moving again. "I've thought about this. I don't just want to be out there. I want to be more than Rudy. If Mr. Dolan ever puts me in the game, I want it to be because he thinks I can help us win."

"What if that doesn't happen this season?" his dad said. "You'll really be okay with that?"

"If I wasn't, I'd quit," Scott said. "And I'm not quitting."

"You don't have to prove anything to anybody," his dad said. "Especially me."

"Maybe I've just got a hard head," he said.

He didn't change out of his uniform when they got home. He ran up the stairs and tossed his helmet on the bed and got his football and took Casey out to Parry Field.

He started by just throwing the ball around, throwing it to an imaginary Jeremy Sharp or even an imaginary Jimmy Dolan. Casey happily—and loudly—chased down the ball, no matter how far it went, and brought it back. Then Scott kicked for a while, first off the tee, then dropkicks after that, stubbornly staying with the dropkicks—that hard head of his again—even though today he couldn't make more than two in a row.

It was still a perfect day for football, sunny and cold, but not too cold, the wind at his back when he faced the goalposts. The field looked perfect, too. The men had just been there the day before to mow it, and Scott had used his roller to chalk the lines when they were through.

When he finally made three dropkicks in a row, he went to the end of the thirty-yard field and tried to pace off another thirty yards.

The length of Grant's run against the Rams.

Now he crouched down behind an imaginary center, started calling out signals.

Not an announcer today, a football player in a football uniform, even if there wasn't a speck of dirt on it.

Casey watched from the sidelines, waiting to see what was going to happen next. As if even Casey the dog wanted to see what play Scott had called.

As soon as Scott pulled back with the ball, he ran to his right. Like Chris on a sweep.

Then he stopped the way Chris had, threw the ball high up in the air, high enough that Scott had time to run under it, throwing the ball to himself the way Chris had thrown it to Grant.

As soon as Scott caught it, he ran for the end zone at Parry Field, Casey falling into place alongside him, Scott really feeling the wind at his back now.

He ran like he was running to win the game, veering a little toward the left sideline the way Grant had on the day when his number finally got called.

Scott ran, feeling his legs pumping hard, feeling the ball tucked securely under his arm, hearing his own breath.

Ran like he was the fastest one on the field.

FOURTEEN

It all started about ten minutes before practice ended, and the funny thing was, it started with Scott finally making a play.

At least he thought he had.

They had gone a little longer than usual Monday night, Mr. Dolan having told them that their next opponent, the Lions, was the best team— besides their own—he had seen in the league.

"I scouted them Saturday afternoon," he said. "And I'm here to tell you boys that we're going to have our work cut out for us."

Scott barely heard the part about them having their work cut out for them. He was stuck on what Mr. Dolan had said right before that, just like how Chris got stuck on words he couldn't sound out.

Thinking to himself: You *scouted* them?

A bunch of sixth-graders?

He felt himself starting to giggle, the way you'd start to giggle in class sometimes without being able to stop yourself, and had to make it sound like he was coughing.

"You okay there, Parry?" Mr. Dolan said.

"Think I might have swallowed a bug, Coach," Scott said.

Then Mr. Dolan was telling them that in addition to the Lions having good players on both offense and defense, and being well-coached, they had also returned two punts for touchdowns in their game against the Giants.

"Let me give you boys a heads-up," he said. "Punt returns like that are *not* happening on Saturday."

They had spent the last half hour of practice covering punt returns as if their lives depended on it, trying to contain Jeremy Sharp. There were a bunch of guys missing that night, because it turned out to be the night when the sixth-graders from Bloomfield South were helping pass out food at a local soup kitchen. So Scott had been in on every play for once, even though his job was the same every time:

Line up opposite Jimmy on the outside and try to slow him down before he went downfield and tried to tackle Jeremy. And, unfortunately for Scott, Jimmy had been taking the job seriously for a change, maybe because he saw how serious his dad was about covering these returns.

It basically meant he wasn't going out of his way to dough-pop Scott every chance he got.

Dave Kepp was their punter. He couldn't place-kick to save his life, but somehow that didn't prevent him from being a really good punter. And tonight it seemed like he was getting even more hang time than usual, giving Jimmy a chance to make one tackle after another.

One time when they were lined up, waiting for Dave to kick again, Jimmy said to Scott, "You know you're catching a break tonight, right, brain? When my old man gets locked in on something like this, even I'm smart enough not to horse around."

"Am I supposed to, like, thank you?" Scott said.

"Don't push it," Jimmy said, then gave Scott another head fake, as if he needed one, and went right around him again. Only this time, Jeremy ran for about twenty yards before Dave Kepp had to run him out of bounds. When the play was over, Mr. Dolan announced that he'd been ready to call it a night, but since Jeremy had nearly broken one, they were going to do it one more time.

"And maybe just this once," Mr. Dolan said, "the outside guys on the return team could be something more than speed bumps for the guys on the kicking team."

He was looking right at Scott when he said it.

"Don't even think about trying to block me, brain," Jimmy said just loud enough for Scott to hear. "Just get out of my way like you always do, or it will *not* be pretty."

Scott didn't say anything back to him, just decided this wasn't going to be a play when he tried to slow Jimmy down, it was going to be a play when he *put* him down.

Sometimes Jimmy would fake to Scott's right, toward the sideline, and then cut inside. Sometimes he would fake Scott to the right and go that way anyway. Waiting for the snap, Scott remembered something his dad said one time when they were playing tennis and Scott was up at the net.

"You might as well guess one way or the other," his dad said. "Because if you just stand there in the middle, the other guy's going to pass you every time."

Scott was tired of getting passed.

He decided to guess.

The brain was finally using his on a football field.

As soon as Jimmy made his head fake this time, Scott moved in the same direction, setting himself good and low for his block, elbows out wide, not caring if Jimmy tried to run right through him, ready to finish his block—something Mr. Dolan talked about all the time—no matter what.

This time Scott was the one initiating the contact.

Just not very well.

• • •

Scott dropped his shoulder and tried to drive it into Jimmy's midsection. But the moment he did get low, Jimmy grabbed Scott by his left shoulder pad, like he wanted to just toss him out of the way.

Even as he started to fall, Scott was determined to finish the block, no matter what.

Somehow he rolled forward as Jimmy tried to step over him, only managing to catch him with his legs.

Instead of being in the clear, Jimmy stepped on Scott's foot. His leg collapsed underneath him, and down he went.

Hard.

As soon as he hit the ground, he was grabbing for his right ankle and yelling at Scott, "You tripped me, you stinking cheater."

Scott said, "No—"

Mr. Dolan was there now, standing over both of them.

"Dad, you saw it," Jimmy said. "He leg-whipped me when I started to go by him."

Mr. Dolan was kneeling next to Jimmy by now.

Mr. Hartung, their assistant coach, had gone to get an ice pack out of their first aid kit.

Mr. Dolan turned, looked up at Scott and said, "We don't block with our legs, Parry. It's against the rules, and it's how people get hurt."

"I was just trying to stay with the block," Scott said.

"Sure you were."

Scott didn't just feel Mr. Dolan's eyes on him.

He felt everyone's.

"Our legs got tangled up," Scott said.

"He's lying!"

Jimmy.

Mr. Dolan, in a low voice, not anything like his coach voice, said to Scott, "You haven't stayed with one block all night."

"I tried to block him, not trip him," Scott said.

"Mr. Dolan," Chris said, stepping forward, "Scott doesn't lie."

Mr. Dolan turned, and now he gave Chris Conlan a long look.

"Did you see the play, Conlan?"

"No, sir. I'm just sayin'—"

"My advice would be to not say anything," Mr. Dolan said.

"He's not good enough to play, so he plays dirty," Jimmy said.

Mr. Dolan was the one holding the ice to his ankle, still staring at Scott. Scott looked around. Everybody was staring at him.

"I didn't mean to hurt anybody," he said, knowing he was sounding lamer by the second.

"Right," Jimmy said. "I tripped myself."

Mr. Dolan helped him to his feet, telling him not to put any weight on his ankle, then saying, "Let's get you home and hope that thing doesn't swell up on you."

Then he looked right at Scott and shook his head, saying, "Your first real contribution of the whole season is getting one of our best players injured."

Then he and Jimmy left without another word and walked toward the parking lot, leaving Scott feeling alone, even with the rest of the team standing there with him.

• • •

Usually Scott would have been getting a ride home from Mrs. Conlan, because it was her night to pick up. But she and Chris were making a quick trip to the mall to get him some new pants for school since he'd already grown out of the ones she'd bought him in the summer.

So Scott's mom was coming to pick him up. She just hadn't shown up by the time Mrs. Conlan and Chris were leaving.

Chris rolled down the window of his mom's car and said, "You sure you're gonna be all right?"

"My mom will be here any second."

"I meant about what happened out there tonight."

"I'm good," he said.

He wasn't.

He sat down on the curb and waited, head down, replaying his block on Jimmy Dolan again and again until he looked up and saw the three of them standing over him.

Bren Mahoney, the team's middle linebacker and Jimmy Dolan's best friend on the team. Charlie Grow, another linebacker. And Quinn Kellogg, who played nose tackle on defense and center on offense.

Bren spoke first.

"You happy now, brain?"

"No," Scott said, not making any move to get up. "Actually, I'm not."

Charlie said, "You know how this could mess us up totally, right? If Jimmy's out for the year?"

"He twisted his ankle, is all," Scott said.

"Oh, now the brain is a doctor," Quinn said.

Scott looked around. It was just the four of them in the parking lot. Everybody else was gone. He seemed to remember Bren saying one time that he lived practically across the street and could walk home.

"Get up when we're talking to you," Bren said.

Scott stood up, not wanting to make this any worse than it already was. "I'm not looking for any trouble," Scott said.

"That's 'cause you made enough already to-night," Bren said.

"We were talking about it after," Charlie said. "How if you weren't a dirty player you wouldn't be any kind of player at all."

"It wasn't a dirty play, and you know it," Scott said.

"I saw the whole thing," Quinn said, "and that's *exactly* what it was."

In a quiet voice, Bren said, "It should've been you that got hurt, not Jimmy."

He was as close to Scott as he could get now without actually touching him. Charlie was to Scott's right, just as close. He could feel Quinn behind him.

"We were all wondering," Bren said, "just when you're going to stop pretending you're a football player?"

Charlie said, "You've got one friend on the whole team, and that's probably just Conlan doing it out of pity."

It was like they were taking turns pushing him around, even without laying a hand on him.

"And if Jimmy can't play," Quinn said, "even he's not gonna want you around."

They all heard the car horn then.

Scott looked between Bren and Charlie and saw his mom's Volvo pulling into the back parking lot.

Still nobody moved.

"I gotta go," Scott said. "My mom's here."

Bren moved back. So did Charlie. Scott started walking toward the car.

"That's it, run to Mommy," Bren said.

Scott kept walking.

"But since you are such a brain," Bren said, "why don't you go home tonight and think of a way to *really* help this team?"

FIFTEEN

They were all in the living room after dinner, television sets off, no calls to be answered on the house phone, his dad's cell phone turned off. Those were the rules for family conferences, and Scott had asked for a family conference once his dad, who'd worked late, had finished his dinner.

Now his parents sat on the couch, waiting.

"I don't want to be on the team anymore," Scott said. "And I don't want you guys to try to change my mind."

His dad smiled. "Doesn't sound like much of a family conference to me. Sounds like a brief opening statement from the president, then no questions."

"Dad, I didn't mean it that way."

His mom said, "Do we at least get to hear why?"

"I was going to," Scott said, and then described what had happened at practice. He tried not to rush through it, wanting to make sure he got it all in so they'd understand what it had been like after Jimmy got hurt, how Chris had tried to stick up for him, how Mr. Dolan had just walked away from him finally, after saying the only thing Scott had done all year was get somebody hurt.

He wasn't going to tell them about what Bren and the other guys had said after practice, because he wasn't going to tell anybody that. There was no way to do that without sounding like the biggest baby in the world.

When he was done telling the story he'd decided to tell, his dad stood up, his face red, saying, "Okay, the conference is over, I'm calling that guy."

But Scott's mom put a hand on his arm and said, "Let's talk about this a little bit."

Scott knew it was her polite, Mom way of telling him he wasn't going anywhere.

Scott said, "We can talk all you want, Mom. I'm still quitting."

"But you've worked so hard," she said.

Scott was standing in the middle of the room, feeling a lot more nervous here than he did when he had to get up in front of the class and say something. "You didn't see how the rest of the guys were looking at me," he said. "Like they all believed Jimmy that the only way I could ever get him down was if I did something dirty. I'm not sure even Chris thought I had it in me to throw a decent block."

"Chris said he believed you, in front of the team," Hank Parry said. "Sounds like at least he told the truth, that you don't lie." He was leaning forward, squeezing both knees with his hands, face even redder than before. "The only people who wouldn't know that are ones who haven't taken the time to find out anything about you, other than deciding you're not going to play for the real Eagles someday."

"Dad, it doesn't matter. If this is all he thinks of me and this is all the other guys—maybe except

Chris—think of me, then what am I doing on this team in the first place?"

"Honey," his mom said, "you don't know that the rest of the players think that. And by the time Mr. Dolan calms down a little—"

"He seemed pretty calm to me," Scott said.

His mom smiled, as if smiling away the fact that he'd interrupted her, and said, "I'm sure twisted ankles happen all the time in sports and don't have to be anybody's fault."

"He probably just wanted to act hurt because he was embarrassed that you finally got the best of him," his dad said.

"Dad, you're not listening," Scott said. "This isn't about Jimmy. It's about me. I'm turning in my uniform tomorrow night."

His parents looked at each other, as if deciding which one would go first. Then Scott saw his mom give his dad the tiniest nod.

Mr. Parry took a deep breath. "I've always taught you to finish what you started, haven't I?"

Scott nodded, not liking where this was going.

"We talk about that a lot, right? Even when it's something like cleaning your room?"

"Dad—"

"Let me finish, okay?"

Another nod, Scott looking his dad in the eyes, because that's what his dad had taught him to do, from as far back as Scott could remember.

Even if you didn't like what they were saying.

"But I've always told your mother I was never going to force you to play sports," he said. "And I certainly don't want sports to ever make you as miserable as you are right now."

Scott just waited.

"But I do want to ask you a question, pal. Are you quitting because you *are* this miserable, or just because you got your feelings hurt tonight?"

"I'm doing it because this is a lost cause," Scott said.

"The season's not over."

"For me it is."

"You can't let this coach run you off, whether you like him or not," his dad said. "I had plenty of coaches like this Dolan guy, believe me."

"Dad," Scott said, "I'm not you."

His dad looked at his mom, then back at Scott. "That's not the problem, son," he said. "The problem is that tonight you're not being you."

Hank Parry stood up, as if saying the conference was over.

"Sleep on it," he said. "If you still want to quit tomorrow, I'll come home early and drive you over to the practice field myself."

Scott hadn't changed his mind by the time he got up in the morning.

All day at school he felt as if he was keeping this huge secret from Chris, but he wasn't ready to talk about it with him, especially not at school, where somebody might overhear them. Not that anybody on the team would really care.

He decided to tell Chris when they were studying together—Scott's house today—later.

They took Chris's bus after school so they could pick up Brett, then Mrs. Conlan drove them all to Scott's, telling Chris she'd see him after practice.

His practice, Scott thought, *not mine.*

Up in his room, with the dogs running around in the backyard, Scott put off telling him a little more. They were working on math today, using a game Scott's mom had bought for them, called "24." Not from the TV show 24. This was like a board game, with all these different cards, four numbers on every one of them, in different combinations. You had to figure out how to use some combination of addition, subtraction, multiplication and division so that you ended up with a total of twenty-four.

Scott was having Chris work without a pencil and paper, saying it would help him organize things better inside his head.

"Just another exercise for his brain," Scott's mom had said.

Sometimes he thought she was into this as much as he was. Like she was the real head coach in this and Scott was just her assistant.

Scott had turned the whole thing into another competition, him against Chris this time, making it more fair by giving himself the hardest combinations, but still doing the thing that Chris understood best: keeping score.

Sometimes Chris would struggle. Sometimes he'd give up entirely and start firing his cards across Scott's room like Frisbees and saying this was a stupid game and math was a stupid subject and he was stupid.

"You want to stop?" Scott said the first time Chris got frustrated today.

"Nah," Chris said. "You know our deal. I just need a twenty." Then he made the motion basketball coaches made, tapping their shoulders with their fingers, when they wanted a twenty-second time-out.

"There's never one easy day," Chris said. "You get that, right?"

"Dude," Scott said, grinning at him, "who ever said this was going to be easy?"

They went back to playing "24" until Chris said his head was going to officially explode and couldn't they please go outside and throw the ball around for a while?

It was the last thing Scott wanted to do today, be anywhere near a football or a football field, but he relented.

On their way through the woods, Scott said, "Don't you ever get tired of playing football?"

"Never."

"You love it that much?"

"That's why you play, dude," Chris said, running toward the field. "Love of the game."

Now, Scott told himself.

You have to tell him now.

When he came out of the woods, Chris was running crazy patterns on the field, the dogs chasing him, barking away as usual. Chris seemed happier to be out here than the dogs, maybe because it meant he was through studying for the day.

Scott walked over to him when he finally stopped and said, "Hey, there's something I need to tell you."

Chris looked at him, as if he knew something. "Please don't tell me you're quitting studying with me."

"No," Scott said, "I'd never do that. But I am quitting football."

Then he went right into why, doing it the way

they had with Chris's parents that time, not giving him a chance to say anything. Scott didn't tell it the way he had last night with his own parents— he skipped a lot of parts because Chris had been there—yet still left out what had happened in the parking lot. He knew that if he told Chris about what Bren and Charlie and Quinn had done, it would just rip the team apart.

"I'm turning in my uniform tonight," Scott said. "It's not like anybody's gonna miss me. The only way Coach ever noticed me was when I got his son hurt."

Then he started running, like he was going out for a pass, putting an arm up the way you did when you were open.

Or maybe he was running away from what he'd just said.

When he was about twenty yards away, Chris Conlan threw a pass so hard that Scott felt like the ball took a couple of fingers with it as it went sailing through his hands.

"Wow," Scott said, forcing a smile even though

his hands really hurt, "where did that missile come from?"

Chris didn't smile back. Just continued to stare at him.

"I don't like quitters," Chris said. "That's where it comes from."

This wasn't Chris his friend now. This wasn't even the Chris who'd called him "brain" in front of Jimmy Dolan.

This was the quarterback.

Scott was getting the kind of look he'd see from Chris on the sidelines after he'd messed up or somebody else on the offense had messed up and the Eagles had either turned the ball over with a fumble or interception or just not made the yardage they needed on fourth down.

A look that made you want to duck.

"Can I say something?"

"No."

"I'm not allowed to explain?"

"You just did. Mr. Dolan and Jimmy hurt your little feelings and so now you're taking your ball and going home."

Maybe it was the tone of his voice, the way he seemed to be mocking the whole thing, but now Scott got mad.

"What are you," he said, "my father?"

"I'm your friend," Chris said. "And I thought you were mine."

"What, I'm not good enough to be your friend now because I'm not a good football player?"

"I'd rather be friends with someone who's not a good player than with a stinking quitter."

"If this is your way of trying to talk me out of it, forget about it," Scott said. Yelling now. "My parents couldn't do it, and neither can you!"

"Who's trying to talk you out of anything?" Chris said. "You do whatever you want, you know everything."

"Fine!" Scott said.

"Fine!"

Scott figured that if they stayed at this for another minute they were going to start making faces at each other.

Or calling each other names.

Chris was the one who broke it off, whistling

for Brett as he started walking back toward the woods.

"How are you going to get to practice?" Scott called after him. "My mom was supposed to take us."

Without turning around, Chris said, "What do you mean, us?"

Before Scott could say anything else, he was already in the woods, Brett following behind him.

Right behind Brett was Casey.

Like somehow even Casey knew what was going on, and even he didn't want to hang around with a quitter today.

Scott thought Casey would come back right away.

He didn't.

He kept waiting for his mom to come walking on the field, wanting to know what had happened.

She didn't.

He'd left his watch up in his room when he and Chris had been studying, so he didn't know what time it was, just knew the sky was starting to look the way it usually did when it was time to leave for practice.

Except there was no practice today.

Scott decided to practice kicking anyway, do something fun, have football be fun the way it used to be out here, before he kidded himself into thinking he could be a real player.

He walked over to the middle of the field, extra-point distance, trying to pretend he was Doug Flutie. Ready to try the Flutie dropkick.

Then he couldn't help it, he could hear his dad's voice inside his brain, telling him for what felt like the thousandth time that no matter how many people tried to tell Flutie he was too small to be a great football player, even when he was in high school, he never gave up.

The way Rudy never gave up.

He kicked the ball now.

Wide right.

No Casey to get the ball. He went and got it himself. Then he walked toward the woods alone, wondering if Doug Flutie or Rudy ever felt as low as he did right now.

He was in his room, door closed, when he heard the car in the driveway, looked out the window and saw it was his dad, coming home early like he'd said he would.

Scott heard the front door close.

Heard his dad calling out in his singsong way, "Honey, I'm home," the way he always did. He had explained that's the way dads did it on TV when he was growing up.

Finally, Scott heard his dad coming up the stairs, then knocking on his door.

"You in there?"

"Yeah."

"All right if I come in?"

"Yeah."

His dad opened the door and as soon as he saw Scott, he broke out into the biggest smile he had, like it was two or three for the price of one.

Scott wasn't only dressed in his uniform, he even had his helmet on.

"I'm ready for practice," he said.

SIXTEEN

In the end, Scott had worked it out for himself, decided it wasn't about Mr. Dolan, or Jimmy, or Chris, or even his parents.

He was playing for himself.

It wasn't as if he didn't want to get out on the field in a real game. Scott still wanted that in the worst way, even if he *was* the worst player on the team.

But if it didn't happen this season, well, he could live with that more than he could live with being a quitter. It wasn't just Chris who didn't want to hang around with a quitter.

Neither do I, Scott thought.

When he got to practice, he thought Chris

might at least act a little surprised to see him, but he didn't.

"Hey," was all he said.

"Hey," Scott said back.

Then Chris nodded and put out his fist and Scott bumped him back, and they went out to stretch along with everybody else.

It turned out Jimmy had a "high ankle sprain." Scott wasn't sure how that was different from any other kind of ankle sprain, but Mr. Dolan said it was the worst kind and he wasn't sure when Jimmy would play again. He was definitely out of Saturday's game against the Lions.

Before they started scrimmaging, he said one other thing, making it sound as if he was addressing the whole team, even though Scott knew better.

"Let's keep it clean tonight, okay?"

They spent most of tonight's practice working on their "red zone" offense, which meant the offense tried to score from inside the other team's twenty-yard line. Sometimes they'd start from the twenty, sometimes first-and-goal from the eight-yard line.

Scott watched every play from the sidelines, as usual.

Finally Mr. Dolan moved the ball back to midfield and told Chris, "Okay, it's first down here, one minute left, no time-outs. Gotta score a touchdown to win the game." If the offense did score, Mr. Dolan told them, the defense would have to to run laps afterward. If the defense held, the guys on offense would run.

As the offense went to huddle up, Mr. Dolan pointed at Scott and told him to get in at cornerback and cover Jeremy.

Scott didn't think he could possibly have heard right.

"What did you say, Coach?"

"I said, I want you to take over at left corner."

"But—" But, he wanted to say, I haven't played one down at cornerback all season.

"Is there a problem, Parry?"

"No, sir." Scott was fumbling around with his fingers, trying to get the strap on his helmet snapped.

"Then get out there."

When Scott got to the defensive huddle, Bren

Mahoney said to him, "We are *not* going to be the ones doing the running after practice. So here's the deal, Parry: If Jeremy starts to blow past you, do what you do best and trip him."

A couple of the other guys laughed.

Bren Mahoney said, "I get why Mr. D wants to pick on you for what you did to Jimmy. But why's he have to pick on us at the same time?"

Mr. Dolan was in the huddle with the offense, calling every play. The first two were passes to Dave Kepp, who had replaced Jimmy at tight end. Dave ran out of bounds both times, the second pass gaining enough yards for a first down.

"Thirty-eight seconds left," Mr. Dolan said, looking at his watch.

When the offense broke the huddle this time, Scott noticed Chris staring right at him, like he was trying to stare a hole right through him, holding the look as he walked up to the line, still looking at him as he bent down to take the snap.

Scott didn't have to run over and ask him what was happening, because he knew.

Practice was about to come straight at him.

• • •

Scott immediately backed up five more yards and wished he could back all the way into the parking lot.

At least Bren Mahoney didn't make it easy for Chris. Bren picked this play to blitz, and it must have surprised Chris's blockers, because nobody picked him up. So as Jeremy Sharp made his cut to the right sideline, Scott could see Chris scrambling away from Bren to his right.

That was the last thing Scott saw as he turned and ran after Jeremy, who was ten yards past him already.

Scott had never rooted against Chris Conlan, but rooted against him now as hard as he could, hoping Bren would run him out of bounds or sack him, that the next thing he'd hear was Mr. Dolan's whistle blowing.

He heard what felt like half the team yelling "Ball!" instead.

Scott knew he was beaten—badly—but also knew that you better turn around when you heard everybody yelling that the ball was in the air.

As he did, he saw the ball coming in his direction end over end, looking more like a punt falling to earth than one of Chris Conlan's perfect spirals.

Whatever had happened, the pass was *way* underthrown.

"Aw, man," he heard Jeremy Sharp say from behind him.

It wasn't Scott fighting to catch up with Jeremy now, it was the other way around, Jeremy trying to come back and give himself a chance to make the catch.

Scott tried to do the same thing, putting the brakes on because he could see he'd nearly outrun the ball himself.

As he did, he got his feet tangled up.

As usual.

He didn't need anybody's help this time. He was just tripping himself up the way he always did, falling backward, unable to stop himself, not sure where Jeremy was in relation to the ball, not really caring.

Two things happened then, one amazing, one not so amazing.

The not-so-amazing thing:

Scott ended up on his butt.

The amazing thing:

The ball ended up in his lap.

He had intercepted the pass.

"You let me get it," Scott said later in the car.

"Did not."

"You threw it to me on purpose."

Chris said, "You think I'd do that on the same day you tried to desert me? Nope. No way."

It was Mrs. Conlan's turn to drive them home after practice. From the front seat now she said, "Please tell me you two aren't going to go on this way all the way to Scott's house."

Her face smiling at them in the rearview mirror.

"We're done," Chris said.

"No, we're not," Scott said, not letting go. "You've never thrown a pass that wobbly in your life."

"How many times do I have to tell you?" Chris said. "Bren hit me just as I released the ball."

"I heard Bren say he hit you right after you released the ball," Scott said.

"Who are you going to believe," Chris said. "Your best friend or Jimmy Dolan's?"

Scott didn't say anything right away.

"I'm waiting," Chris said.

"I believe you," Scott said, adding, "I guess."

They were pulling into his driveway by then. Scott thanked Mrs. Conlan for the ride and reminded Chris that they were studying together tomorrow even though there were teacher conferences, which meant no school.

Chris said, "So now I have school even when there's no school."

"Pretty much," Scott said.

"Am I a lucky guy, or what?" Chris said.

Scott walked through the front door smiling, thinking it was funny how things worked out, how what had started out to be one of the worst days of his life had turned with him making that pick on Jeremy. How when the season started, he would have given anything to make a play like that, even in practice.

But that wasn't what had him smiling.

He knew that one play wasn't going to change things, not really.

No.

What had him smiling was that Chris Conlan had called him his best friend.

SEVENTEEN

The Eagles beat the Lions the next Saturday even without scoring an offensive touchdown, even without Jimmy, their best blocker on offense and their best tackler on defense. Bren Mahoney ran back an interception all the way for one score, Jeremy Sharp returned the second half kickoff for a touchdown, and the final score was 12–6.

No extra points in the game. Nobody ever even tried to kick in their league, the teams always went for two points, but today nobody had been able to convert after any of the touchdowns.

Jimmy showed up for the game on crutches, though Scott noticed he was moving around pretty well without them a couple of times when he thought nobody was watching him.

Scott did a good job of avoiding him for most of the game, but with two minutes to go, Jimmy came over and stood next to him.

"Good game, brain," he said. Then, "Oops, my bad. I guess you didn't get in."

Scott moved away from him.

Jimmy, hopping on his crutches, moved with him. "Ask you a question, brain?"

There was no way to avoid this guy, on the field or off. "Sure," Scott said. "Why not?"

Jimmy said, "Why are you still here?"

"You mean why am I still here having a conversation with you?"

"You know what I mean. Why are you even on this team?"

Scott said, "None of your business."

"You don't do anything," Jimmy continued. "The only guy on the team who likes you is Chris. So why don't you just quit?"

Scott felt himself clenching his fists, trying to decide what hurt more, that Jimmy was saying these things or that he was saying all the things Scott had thought about himself all season, even after he made up his mind not to do what Jimmy wanted him to do.

He turned and looked at Jimmy.

"I'm sort of wasting my time here," Scott said, "because I'm gonna tell you something you're not going to understand."

Jimmy frowned, not sure if he was being insulted or not.

"Watch it, brain. I only need one good leg to kick your butt."

"Yeah, I know how tough you are. But even you have to know by now that if you knock me down, I'll get back up."

"Whatever. You still haven't answered my question."

"Sometimes," Scott said, "guys love the game even if it doesn't love them back."

Now Scott walked away, walked down the sideline and cheered for Chris and the rest of the guys on offense as they tried to run out the clock.

For once, Jimmy didn't follow.

• • •

Scott and Chris made a deal:

No matter what happened, in football or study-ing, neither one of them was going to talk about quitting the rest of the way.

Then they shook on it with a handshake Chris had invented, one so complicated Scott was sure he was changing it every time they shook on some-thing, palms up, palms down, up high, down low, even a shoulder bump at the end.

Scott was going to work harder than ever on the practice field between now and the end of the season. Chris was going to work harder than ever in the study sessions they had left before his equiva-lency test, scheduled now for the Monday after the championship game.

With one game left in the regular season, they were 5–0 and had locked up the number-one seed. If the Lions, whose only loss had been to the Ea-gles, won their last game, they were going to finish number two and play the Eagles for the title.

"The football season feels like it just started,"

Chris said, "but, dude, my *study* season feels like it's gone on forever."

"You're doing better than you ever thought you would."

"I don't stink as much as I used to, put it that way."

This was Friday afternoon, before practice. They'd finished studying, working only on English today, mixing up reading and writing. Scott didn't let Chris get up now when something had him stumped—he explained that Chris wouldn't be able to get up and walk around the room and even toss a ball to himself if he got stumped during the equivalency test. It didn't work like that.

Now they were out having another kicking contest on Parry Field, Scott winning the way he always did, especially when they got around to drop-kicking.

As good as Chris Conlan was at everything else at football, he just couldn't kick to save his life.

"Someday," Chris said, "when we get to high school, you're going to be our star kicker."

"Dream on, sucker."

"No, seriously," Chris said. "Just because Mr. Dolan has no use for kickers doesn't mean every coach you're ever gonna have is gonna feel the same way."

"Yeah," Scott said, "because I'm going to have so many football coaches in my life."

"You wait."

Scott squared up and drop-kicked one through from twenty yards away.

"Look at that," Chris said. "Plenty of distance. Center cut all the way."

"Yeah," Scott said. "Very useful. Being able to drop-kick is like being able to eat a whole blueberry pie."

Chris tried to match him, nearly kicked the ball sideways, then just stood there laughing at himself, looking totally helpless.

Like he was a brain trying to be good at football.

"But if they ever do bring back the dropkick—" Chris said.

"I'll be the first one picked in the draft."

"Oh, yeah," Chris said. "You'll be a wild man."

"Wild man" being one of their favorite expressions from *Rudy*, when Rudy's buddy is yelling "Who's a wild man now?" as the other Notre Dame players carry Rudy off the field.

"Trouble is," Scott said, "it's hard to be a wild man if you can't get into a game."

Even Chris had to admit that was a good point.

Mr. Dolan dropped his bombshell that night when they got to practice.

"Everybody plays tomorrow," he said as they were stretching.

Just like that.

"And when I say play," he continued, walking in between the players, "I mean that even the guys who haven't gotten to do much this season are going to get their hands on the ball."

As excited as Scott was, he couldn't help thinking: *Haven't gotten to do much?*

How about haven't gotten to do anything?

He didn't know why the change of heart and he didn't care. The way he didn't care that tomorrow's opponent, the Panthers, was the worst team in their league, one without a win or even a touchdown.

He was finally getting into a game.

"You think he really means it?" Scott said to Chris when they were jogging around the outside of the field.

"Say what you want about the guy," Chris said, "but *he* says what he means."

So for the first time, the first time *for real,* Scott got to work with the starters on offense. Got real "reps" as Mr. Dolan called them. Not just a play or two at the end of practice, but for whole drives. Most of the time he was out at wide receiver. A couple of times Chris even threw the ball his way. Once Scott was wide open, but Chris, probably trying to give him a pass he could handle, threw the ball way too easy and it floated so far out of Scott's reach that Jimmy Dolan— whose ankle was better—nearly intercepted it.

When Scott got back to the huddle after that one, Chris's face had turned its mad shade of red.

"I am such a jerk," he said. "I aimed the sucker instead of just throwing it."

"It's cool."

"No, it's not cool," Chris said.

Then he called for the reverse.

To Scott.

"I don't know about this," Scott said.

"I do," Chris said. "Once you get around the corner, you're gonna see nothing but green grass."

Chris turned after taking the snap from center, faked the ball to Grant up the middle, started to run to his left so the defense would follow him. As he did, Scott came running from where he'd split out to the left and Chris casually stuck the ball in his belly.

"Go," Chris said as he did.

Scott made sure he didn't drop it, looked up, turned the corner, and saw nothing but open field in front of him.

Nothing but green grass.

It was as if everybody on the left side of the defense had gone home early.

Scott knew he didn't have the speed to go all the way. But for these few seconds, it didn't matter. He was in the clear, like he was alone with Casey on Parry Field.

For these few seconds, this was the season he had dreamed about.

Even if it was only practice.

He allowed himself one quick look back as he headed down the sidelines, just to check where the defense was. He found out soon enough. Because there came Jeremy Sharp, making up ground as if Scott were standing still.

Scott turned back around, put his head down, kept running, putting both hands on the ball now, promising himself that no matter what, he was *not* dropping this ball, even if Jeremy tried to take his head off.

Jeremy, one of the nicest kids on the team, didn't try to do that, as it turned out. When he caught up with Scott at the twenty-yard line, he just gave him enough of a shove to push him out of bounds.

Jeremy wasn't the problem.

The problem was that Jimmy was right behind him. Scott didn't know that, the way he didn't know what hit him as soon as he was out of bounds.

Just knew that he was suddenly airborne, that the ball was flying out of his hands right before he hit the ground and felt his left wrist explode.

EIGHTEEN

Scott didn't know his dad was there.

But he was.

So his dad's voice was the first one Scott heard, even though he was still facedown, afraid to take his left arm out from under him, that was how much it hurt.

The only thing that kept him from crying was this:

He was a football player.

In a gentle voice, his dad said, "See if you can roll over."

Then in a completely different voice, one Scott barely recognized, he heard his dad say, "Get away from my son, Coach. Go talk to yours, maybe ask him what he was thinking."

Mr. Dolan said, "Jimmy said he didn't hear the whistle."

"Because he didn't want to," Hank Parry said.

"You're saying he did it on purpose?"

"You're not the only one here who played football, Coach," Scott's dad said. "By the way, if it isn't too much trouble, I could use some ice."

Scott rolled over now, used all the strength he had to sit up, keeping the injured wrist pressed to his stomach. His dad unsnapped his helmet, carefully took it off.

"Hey, Dad," Scott said.

"Hey, bud."

"You didn't tell me you were coming to practice."

"Good thing I did come, or I wouldn't have seen you turn into Reggie Bush." Then his dad said, "Let's have a look."

Scott put out his left hand. As he did, he motioned for his dad to come closer and whispered, "It hurts, Dad. A lot."

"Nice and easy, now, let's see how much you can move it."

Scott gently tried moving his wrist up and down, then side to side, surprised that moving it around this way didn't make it hurt more.

"How's that feel?"

"Not great."

"But not any worse than before?"

"No."

"I'm no doctor," his dad said, covering the wrist with his hand now, putting a little pressure on the sides, "but I don't think you broke anything. But the sucker is starting to swell up already."

Mr. Dolan came back with the ice, handed it to Scott's dad. Scott thought Mr. Dolan wanted to say something. But there was something in the look Scott's dad gave him that made him just walk away, as if his dad had glared him away. "I'll call later," Mr. Dolan said, "to see how he's doing."

"Do that," Hank Parry said.

He wrapped the ice pack around Scott's wrist, told him to hold it tight, no matter how cold it got. Then he helped his son to his feet.

As he did, the rest of the Eagles began to applaud.

• • •

It wasn't broken.

His dad had driven him straight to the emergency room. And even though his dad had said they might have to wait, it must have been a slow night there, because the nurse took him in right away to get x-rayed. They took pictures of the wrist from all angles.

After the x-rays had been developed, Dr. Accorsi showed Scott the injured area on the outside, said it was a combination of bone bruise and sprain, had him move it around a little more. Then he told Scott that just to be on the safe side, he was going to put a soft cast on it for a couple of days.

"But I've got a game tomorrow!" Scott said.

The doctor smiled. "Your team does, but I'm afraid you don't."

"It's the last game of the regular season," Scott said, as if that was somehow going to change the doctor's mind.

Dr. Accorsi looked at Scott's dad, then back at Scott. "The good news is that the wrist will be as good as new in a couple of weeks," he said. "The bad news is that you've already played your last game of the regular season."

Scott waited until he got in the car.

Then the football player started to cry.

Chris called in the morning to see how he was doing, ask if Scott was coming to the Panthers game.

"My wrist is still killing me," Scott said, even though it felt much better. "I think I'll sit this one out."

"Come on," Chris said. "After the game we'll go hang out at my house."

"Nah," Scott said. "Watching a game I was going to get into will hurt even more than my wrist does."

That much was the truth. The kind his dad sometimes called the painful truth. Scott didn't want to watch the Eagles crush the Panthers, didn't want to watch another guy off the bench getting carries he would have gotten today, didn't want to go there and act like he was still a part of the team when his season was over.

He'd go to the championship game next Saturday, just to root for Chris. Not because he had to. Because he wanted to. If your best friend was playing for the championship, well, that wasn't a game you could miss.

Today's game he could miss.

After he hung up the phone, he got his ball and whistled for Casey. His parents were in the kitchen having coffee. His dad looked up when he saw Scott with the football. "Hey," he said, "I don't think you should be running around with that wrist today."

Scott said, "I'm just gonna kick. Case will do the running around."

They walked out to Parry Field. In an hour or so, the Eagles would be playing the Panthers.

I was gonna get in the game, he thought.

I was gonna play.

He walked slowly to the end of the field, where the goalposts were, Casey right behind him, ready to chase.

The two of them were right back where they started.

Like this was the only game in town.

NINETEEN

When the doorbell rang the next Saturday morning, the morning of the Eagles' championship game against the Lions, Scott said he'd get it.

He didn't look outside to see who it was, just opened the door and there was Chris, already dressed for the game except for his helmet.

"I told you on the phone I'd see you over there," Scott said.

"Go suit up."

"No," Scott said. "We talked about this yesterday."

"That was before your cast came off."

"Who told?"

"I can't reveal my source," he said, then grinned. "Okay, your mom told my mom."

Dr. Accorsi had taken it off the day before, then

wrapped the wrist in an Ace bandage, saying that was more of a reminder for him to be careful with it than anything else.

"I don't have to be in uniform to watch from the sidelines," Scott said.

"Suit up. We're gonna finish what we started."

"Yeah, with me watching and you playing."

"No," Chris said. "As teammates."

He brushed past Scott and headed up the stairs. "I'm not leaving until you suit up."

"Are you gonna be this stubborn about passing that test on Monday?" Scott said.

"More," he said. "Now come on, or you're gonna make me late."

"I give up," Scott said, and followed him.

He and Chris were coming down the stairs, Chris in his number four—for Brett Favre—and Scott in his number twenty-two for Doug Flutie, when Scott's mom and dad came back from their walk.

His dad just gave him one of those smiles, the kind where he didn't have to say anything because the smile said everything.

"I figured I'm gonna get rained on anyway," Scott said. "I might as well do it wearing this."

"Sounds like a plan," his dad said.

It had started raining earlier that morning, not a big storm, just a steady downpour. Even if it stopped right now, the game was going to be played on a muddy field.

Scott's dad said, "Your mom, Casey and I will see you over there."

Sure enough, the field was a mess by the time the game started.

Yet the first half of the championship game was an even bigger mess.

By then it was no longer just a nice, steady rain, it was a total downpour, but because the coaches had agreed to start the game, they were determined to finish it, no matter how miserable the conditions had become.

Chris fumbled the ball away twice in the first quarter, both times deep in Eagles' territory, but both times the Eagles' defense held, and the game remained scoreless. It looked as if that might change when the Lions' quarterback fumbled on his own twenty-yard line with less than a minute left in the half. Except then Jeremy fumbled right back.

The game was still scoreless at halftime.

For the first time all season, Mr. Dolan took them inside at the break. It wasn't so they could get a chance to get dry. That, they all knew, wasn't happening until they got home. But at least it was fifteen minutes out of the rain.

"You guys are playing your hearts out, and I'm proud of you," Coach said. "I know the conditions are lousy, but they're lousy for the other guys, too." He took off his red cap with the O on the front now, shook it hard to get some of the rain off it.

Then he knelt down in the front of the room where they all could see him.

"This is one you win," he said. "This is one you win and then no matter what you do in football after this, you'll remember this day, and talk about it for the rest of your lives."

Chris stood up then. He wasn't much of a talker, and had never given a speech to the team, but he said something now.

"Let's win the Mud Bowl!" he yelled.

Suddenly all of the Eagles were chanting *"Mud, mud, mud."* Scott was yelling right along with everybody else, knowing they sounded as if they had water on the brain by now.

He and Chris were the last two out of the room as they filed out. "Glad you came?" Chris said.

Scott grinned. "Let's go win the championship," he said.

It didn't get any easier in the second half. Both teams kept turning the ball over. Nobody came close to putting it in the end zone.

Then, near the end of the third quarter, disaster struck for the Eagles.

Dave Kepp was back to punt from his own five-yard line. Only the snap went sailing over his head like it had been shot out of a cannon and landed in the Eagles' end zone. There was a wild scramble for the ball, and for a moment Scott was worried that somebody on the Lions was going to recover it for a touchdown.

At the last second, though, Dave was smart enough to shove the ball out of the back of the end zone for a safety. No touchdown, but now the Lions had a 2–0 lead. And in these conditions, those two points felt like more.

A lot more.

Maybe the whole game.

Because of the safety, the Eagles had to kick the ball back to the Lions, who weren't taking any chances now that they had the lead. They just ran the ball up the middle three straight times from midfield and then watched as their punter boomed one out of bounds on the Eagles' fifteen-yard line. Those eighty-five yards to the Lions' end zone had never looked farther.

On first down, trying to make something happen despite lousy field position that matched the weather, Chris went back to throw one to Jimmy in the right flat. Only the ball slipped out of his hand and somehow ended up behind Chris, falling right into the arms of a Lions' defensive tackle, who seemed as shocked as anybody to have the ball in his hands, then started slip-sliding toward the end zone until Chris managed to bring him down from behind.

Lions' ball, on the Eagles' eight-yard line.

But Scott watched as his guys on defense finally caught a break. The Lions' quarterback fumbled the snap on first down and the Eagles got it back just as the third quarter ended. One last quarter to go in the season.

Lions 2. Eagles 0. A baseball score for the biggest football game of the year, the biggest game any of those kids had ever played.

The rain was coming as hard as ever.

Somehow, though, with three minutes left, Chris Conlan—maybe because he *was* Chris Conlan—began to drive the Eagles down the field.

You couldn't see the numbers on the uniforms by then. You wondered how Chris could see anything with the rain hitting him in the face. Didn't seem to matter to him. He completed his first pass of the day, to Jimmy, and Jimmy nearly dropped it before hugging it to his chest with both hands and running twenty more yards, almost in slow motion to avoid slipping in the mud. The Lions' defenders could hardly plant their feet in the mud to make the tackle.

That gave Chris an idea. He called for the reverse that he'd run with Scott at practice, and Jeremy Sharp gained another fifteen yards.

The Eagles were at midfield now. The element of surprise seemed to be working. On the sloppy field, it was more difficult to react than act. So Chris kept the surprises coming by calling a quarterback sneak and running all the way to the Lions' fifteen-yard line.

One minute to go. The Eagles' first real drive of the game.

Chris called their first time-out, went over to talk to Mr. Dolan.

"No turnovers," he said. "This is for the game."

"Got it," Chris said.

Scott had come over to listen.

"Let's see if we can run it in," Mr. Dolan said. "We've seen already that bad things are happening today when the ball's in the air."

Chris nodded. Scott handed him a bottle of Gatorade. Chris tipped his helmet back to take a swig, and it was then that Scott saw that he was smiling. Like there was nowhere else in the world he'd rather be.

He tossed the bottle to Scott. Still smiling, he said, "Love of the game, dude."

Then the quarterback ran back on the field.

The next play was a sweep. Jeremy ran for three yards. When the play started, it looked like he might get more, but Jeremy fell down without being touched, body-surfing for about five yards after he hit the ground.

Second-and-seven.

They lined up without a huddle to save time. Chris faked a pitch to Jeremy, handed the ball to Grant. But the Lions weren't fooled this time, and Grant got stuffed for no gain.

Third down now, from the twelve-yard line.

Fifteen seconds left.

Chris called another time-out to stop the clock. It was third-and-long. Pass coming. Chris took the snap, rolled to his right. As he did, Scott looked down the field and saw that Jimmy had gotten himself wide open in the back of the end zone, his man having slipped.

It looked like a sure touchdown to win the game.

Except.

Except as Chris's arm came forward, his back foot slipped out from under him and he went down, the ball squirting out of his hand, dying like somebody had shot it out of the air. It fell harmlessly to the ground.

Fourth down from the twelve.

Eight seconds left.

Time for one more play.

Only Chris Conlan was limping now, limping badly, grabbing for his hamstring, in obvious pain. Even with the clock stopped because of the incompletion, he called their last time-out and hobbled toward the sideline.

Mr. Dolan ran out to meet him.

By the time Mr. Dolan had met him halfway, Chris was doubled over, unable to walk. Mr. Dolan leaned over now, put a hand on Chris's shoulder, his face grim, and said something to him. Chris shook his head. Scott got as close as he could, tried to make out what they were saying. The rain was too loud, and they were too far away.

Chris was still bent over. But he turned now and met Scott's eyes, before pointing right at him.

Mr. Dolan took off his cap despite the soaking rain, and rubbed his forehead. Scott thought the coach looked lost for a moment, Chris still speaking at his side.

Then, as if suddenly remembering where he was, Mr. Dolan put his cap back on.

"Parry!" he yelled, his eyes looking everywhere except at Scott. "You're in!"

It took Scott a second to realize what he'd just heard. When he did, he began shaking his head no. But Chris caught his eye again and nodded.

Then Chris, straightening up now, waved him over.

Scott ran toward them.

"Are you crazy?" he said to Chris. "What the heck did you say to Coach?"

"I told him about our secret weapon," Chris said. "Like he said, you're going in."

"To do what?"

"Kick for it," Chris said.

Scott waited for some sign that he was joking,

even with eight seconds left in the championship game. Only he wasn't. He meant this. This was what he'd been talking about with Mr. Dolan, what he'd just spent nearly the whole time-out talking him into.

Scott couldn't talk now, couldn't move, just stood there shaking his head.

"No," he managed finally, still shaking his head. "No way. I can't."

"Yes, you can."

Then Chris Conlan was grabbing Scott by both sides of his helmet, forcing him to focus. "Let's go win a championship," he said.

TWENTY

"This is insane," Scott said.

"Nah," Chris said, "it's Parry Field. Just muddier."

They were standing in front of Mr. Dolan now. The whole team had gathered behind them, wanting to know what was going on. Mr. Dolan said to Scott, "You can do this?"

Chris answered before Scott could. "Coach, he can do it. I know he can even better than he does. It's not just our best chance to win—it's our *only* chance. You saw what just happened when Jeremy was in the clear. And I couldn't throw a pass to save my life even on two good legs."

Mr. Dolan ignored Chris. He tipped back his

cap just slightly. Now Scott could see his eyes, staring at him.

"I'm asking you," he said to Scott. "Can you make this kick?"

"Yes," Scott said, "I can."

The ref came over to where they were standing. "Coach, I've been giving extra time on the whistles. But you gotta get these kids lined up soon or I'm gonna have to call a delay of game on you."

Mr. Dolan nodded. The ref left. When Mr. Dolan started talking again, it was as if he were talking to himself.

"This is nuts," he said. Then looked back at Scott and said, "Go for it."

Jimmy Dolan had been over on the sidelines, trying to clean some of the mud out of his spikes, so he didn't know what they'd been talking about.

"Go for what, Dad?"

"We're gonna kick for it," Mr. Dolan said.

"Who's gonna kick for it?"

Mr. Dolan said, "Scott."

"You're gonna let the brain try a field goal?"

Jimmy said. "Tell me you're joking. *Please* tell me you're joking."

Mr. Dolan gave his son a long look and said, "Tell me something, son. Do I look like I'm joking?"

Scott ignored them, turned to Chris instead.

"You've gotta come out, right?"

Chris nodded.

"So who's going to hold for me?" Scott said.

"It's like I just finished telling Coach," Chris said. "We're not gonna need a holder. It's just one more thing that could go wrong." He paused and said, "That's why you're gonna drop-kick it."

Scott felt the air come out of him the way it had that time Jimmy'd hit him in practice and he was afraid he was never going to catch his breath, the day he'd somehow held on to the ball.

"I can't drop-kick a field goal," he said, choking the words out.

"Would somebody mind telling me what a *drop-kick* is?" Jimmy said.

His dad said, "It's like a punt, except you drop it on the ground before you kick it."

"But it counts the same as a placekick?" Jimmy said.

"Only if you make it," Scott said in a weak voice.

"Look at me!" Chris said, snapping at him. This time he grabbed Scott by the shoulder pads. "You've made this kick with me a hundred times. And every single time it was to win the game. So go make it again."

Then Chris put an arm around Mr. Dolan's shoulder and limped toward the sideline as the rest of the Eagles walked out to huddle.

"I never snapped the ball for a field goal before," Jimmy said. "Just punts."

"Just snap it like that," Scott said. "That's how far back I'll be."

They all heard the ref blow the whistle. Scott looked over and saw the ref's arm come down, which meant he was starting the play clock.

Thirty seconds to run a play.

Scott could see everybody else in the huddle staring now. Staring at him. He took a deep breath and said to all of them, "Block better than you ever have in your lives," before clapping his hands and saying, "on two!"

He carefully paced off eight yards, found a place where there actually seemed to be some grass left.

Scott checked his footing then, alone in the backfield.

Heard somebody on the defense yell, "Trick play!"

They had no idea.

Scott was afraid he'd drop the snap. Or that it would be a bad snap.

Or that he'd slip.

"Ten seconds," the ref said.

In that moment, Scott looked to the right of the goalposts, on the other side of the end zone, and saw his dad standing there.

With Casey.

Like this was Parry Field.

The only place where he was never afraid.

"Hut one," he said.

"Hut two!"

Barking the last word out the way Chris did.

Jimmy Dolan gave him a perfect snap. Scott planted his left foot, not slipping even a little bit, dropped the ball perfectly in the spot he'd cleared, brought his right leg through.

The wet ball felt as if it weighed more than he did, like he was trying to kick a big rock.

As well as he'd hit it, he was sure when it got in the air that it was going to be short.

It wasn't.

It cleared the crossbar with a couple of feet to spare.

Plenty of distance, center cut.

Eagles 3, Lions 2.

The last thing Scott saw before his teammates mobbed him was Casey breaking free from his dad, running after the ball.

TWENTY-ONE

Scott and Chris would talk about it a little more until one of them would start laughing all over again.

"I still don't believe we pulled it off."

"*We* didn't do anything. *You* did."

"I still can't believe it."

"I told you all along you could do it. What, you didn't believe me? That hurts me, dude, I'm not gonna lie."

"I believed that *you* believed. I just wasn't sure I did."

"You did it, that's all that matters. You came through when it counted like I knew you would."

"I still can't believe I passed," Chris said.

They weren't talking this morning about what

was already known at school, all over their town, as The Kick. They were talking about The Test.

There wasn't much more to say about The Kick. They'd gone on about it all week, the way everybody else in town had. They'd even gotten to watch it on SportsCenter, courtesy of Mr. Conlan.

Even in the rain, he'd decided to bring his video recorder with him to the game, hoping something might happen that would be worth keeping.

It wasn't just people in their town who got to see The Kick. The whole country did, on YouTube before it even showed up on ESPN. Which was why on Wednesday of that week, Scott's dad handed him the phone and said, "An old friend of mine wants to talk to you."

Then Scott heard Doug Flutie introducing himself and saying, "Couldn't have done better myself."

So the whole week had been dominated by The Kick. And that was a good thing, because it was a way for Scott and Chris not to spend all their free time worrying about how Chris had done on The Test.

And now they knew.

He'd passed.

Now he and Scott were out on Parry Field with the dogs.

"I'm gonna say this for the last time, and then I promise I won't say it again," Chris said. "I couldn't have done it without you."

"Works for me," Scott said. "Because I wouldn't have even gotten a chance to kick without you."

Chris smiled a cocky quarterback's smile. "Told you I'd get you better at football."

"Told you I'd get you better at school," Scott said.

Then Scott held up a finger, as if he'd just realized something.

"Wait a second," he said. "I could kick before I met you."

"Yeah," Chris said. "In your dreams."

Then Scott snatched the ball away from Chris for a change, and went tearing off with it down the field. Then Chris was tearing after him, and the dogs, thinking this was *their* big game, were after both of them, and the only sound louder than the barking on Parry Field was the sound of more laughter.

ABOUT THE AUTHOR

Mike Lupica, over the span of his successful career as a sports columnist, has proven that he can write for sports fans of all ages and stripes. Now, as the author of multiple hit novels for young readers, including *Travel Team* and *Heat,* both of which went to #1 on the *New York Times* bestseller list, Mr. Lupica has carved out a niche as the sporting world's finest storyteller. Mr. Lupica's column for New York's *Daily News* is syndicated nationally, and he can be seen weekly on ESPN's *The Sports Reporters*. He lives in Connecticut with his wife and four children.

Hooray
for
Anna
Hibiscus!

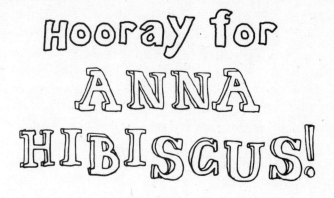

Hooray for ANNA HIBISCUS!

by Atinuke

illustrated by Lauren Tobia

Kane Miller
A DIVISION OF EDC PUBLISHING

First American Edition 2010
Kane Miller, A Division of EDC Publishing

First published in 2008 by Walker Books Ltd., London (England)
Text © 2008 Atinuke
Illustrations © 2008 Lauren Tobia

Library of Congress Control Number: 2009943492

Printed and bound in the United States of America
1 2 3 4 5 6 7 8 9 10
ISBN: 978-1-935279-74-7

To my sisters,
OE and TJ, the original
Double and Trouble
A.

To all the babies,
Hannah, Max, Billy, Finn,
Niamh and Ciara
L.T.

Anna 'biscus! Sing!

Anna Hibiscus lives in Africa. Amazing
Africa. She lives with her mother and her
father; her grandmother and her grandfather;
her aunties and her uncles; her cousins,
little, medium and big; and her twin baby
brothers, Double and Trouble. They all live
together in a big white house.

Anna Hibiscus stays at home all day long with the little cousins. Little cousins do not go to school. They help their mothers and aunties with the work of the big white house, and they play in the beautiful, flower-filled garden.

Anna Hibiscus loves helping her mother and her aunties wash clothes. She loves feeding the chickens and climbing the mango trees to pick the sweet fruit. But especially and particularly, Anna Hibiscus loves singing. She loves singing to her brothers, Double and Trouble, all day long.

Double and Trouble are still babies. They are only just now saying something. They have three new words that Anna Hibiscus is always listening out for.

Trouble's two words are "Anna 'biscus!"

And Double's word is "Sing!"

And if ever they are confused, if ever they are bored or tired, Double and Trouble shout:

"Anna 'biscus!"

"Sing!"

And Anna comes running from wherever she is to sing to her brothers. Because Anna Hibiscus loves her brothers, and Anna Hibiscus loves to sing.

This Christmas, for the very first time,
Anna Hibiscus will see snow – in Canada!
So she sings about snow:

"Snow, you are wonderful!
I will see and tell you so!
Snow, you are so cold-o!
I will feel and say you so!
Snow, you are so sweet-o!
I will taste and tell you so!"

All day long while Anna is singing and playing at home, her father and the uncles and some of the aunties are working hard in their offices and businesses and churches to make Africa a Better Place.

One day Anna Hibiscus's father came home from work. "I want to talk to you, Anna Hibiscus," he said. "I need to explain something important. You are still small, but you are growing bigger every day. You are growing up! And growing-up children have work to do. Work to make Africa – and the whole entire world – a Better Place."

"What work, Papa?" Anna Hibiscus asked.

"It is this," Anna Hibiscus's father said. "Now you are growing up, you must go to school."

Anna Hibiscus was sad. She did not want to go to school where she knew nobody and nobody knew her (except for a few cousins). She did not want to leave the big white house.

But the next school day, her mother
came to call her, and Anna Hibiscus was
very brave. She got up early and put on
a clean school uniform that used to belong
to her big cousin Clarity and said goodbye
to Grandmother and Grandfather and her
mother and her father and the aunties and
the uncles and the little cousins and the
chickens and the goats and the mango trees
and the big white house and the beautiful
garden and Double Trouble, and squeezed
into the car with all the other growing-up
cousins and went to school.

All morning while she was at school, Anna Hibiscus missed everybody and everything in the big white house and the beautiful, wide compound. But most especially and enormously, she missed Double Trouble. She was so far away she could not hear them say, "Anna 'biscus! Sing!" So every outside break time, Anna Hibiscus sang as loudly as she could in the direction of the big white house, just in case they could hear her.

One night when Anna Hibiscus's mother
and father and aunties and uncles came back
from their work, they were full of talk. They
called all the cousins and the stay-at-home
aunties and Grandmother and Grandfather
and told everybody that for the very first time,
the president of a country outside of Africa
was coming to visit their own country.

"Ours is only one of many countries in
Africa," began Uncle Tunde.

"We must show this president how
wonderful our country is," Auntie Joly said.

"And how important things are here,"
Anna's father added.

"But most important of all," Grandfather said
gently, "this president will be our guest. We
must make sure she is comfortable and at ease."

"Then, when she goes away," Grandmother
said, "she will have only kind-hearted feelings
towards our country and our people."

Everybody agreed.

At school the next day, everybody was talking about the same thing.

Anna Hibiscus's teacher announced, "There will be a big welcoming ceremony in the National Stadium for the visiting president. Our school has been asked to participate. We must send a good speaker, a good dancer and a good singer."

She chose a good speaker and a good dancer, and then she said, "Hands up who can sing."

Many children's hands went up. They all wanted to sing in the National Stadium for the important president. Anna Hibiscus sat on her hands. She did not want to sing in front of the president. What if she did not like Anna's song? Then she would go away with no good feelings for Anna's country. And it would all be the fault of Anna and her useless song.

The teacher looked at the children. She had never heard them sing. She did not know who to pick.

Then Anna's cousin Angel said, "Anna Hibiscus can sing!"

"Yes! Yes!" everybody shouted. "It is true! It is true! Anna Hibiscus is singing all the time."

The teacher made Anna Hibiscus stand up. "Sing, Anna," she said.

Anna Hibiscus stood up. She did not
know what to sing.

"Sing 'Snow,'" Angel whispered.

So Anna Hibiscus sang her favorite song
about snow.

"It is true," said the teacher, when Anna
had finished. "Anna Hibiscus, you can sing!
We will send you!"

Back at the big white house, Chocolate and Angel told everybody, "Anna Hibiscus is going to sing for the visiting president!"

"What is this?" everybody asked Anna.

"It is true," Anna Hibiscus said. "My school is going to send me to sing for the president."

"At the National Stadium!" said Chocolate.

"She is going to sing all on her own!" said Angel.

Anna Hibiscus felt very sorry for herself. Double and Trouble looked at her worried face. They felt worried too. "Anna 'biscus! Sing! Anna 'biscus! Sing!" they shouted.

So Anna Hibiscus sang for them until she felt much better.

And now Anna did not mind going to school so much. She did not do mathematics and spelling anymore. She only sang and sang and sang her new president song!

And in the afternoon when she got home, Double Trouble shouted, "Anna 'biscus! Anna 'biscus! Sing! Sing!"

And Anna Hibiscus sang her new president song.

And at night when Double and Trouble
went to bed, Anna Hibiscus sang it to them
again. It was their new favorite song!

"Welcome to our beautiful country,
  Welcome to our wonderful land.
Welcome to the sun shining brightly,
  Welcome to our cool evening rain..."

Morning, noon and
night, Anna Hibiscus
sang this song. She did
not tire of singing it.
It was *her* new
favorite song too.

Anna Hibiscus was happy singing at school and at home. But one day she went to practice at the National Stadium, and she was not happy anymore. The stage was as big as a soccer field. There were thousands of seats in front and all around. Anna felt very small on that stage. She felt as small as an ant. An ant standing alone under World Cup lights.

"Don't worry," said Chocolate, when
Anna came home, "we will be there. It will
be us sitting there. Don't be afraid."

"Don't worry," said Angel. "You know you
can sing. We all know you can sing."

"Sing! Sing!" said Double happily, and
Trouble clapped his hands.

On the night the president arrived, everybody in Anna Hibiscus's family was there waiting at the National Stadium. Her mother and her father and all of their friends. Her grandmother and her grandfather and all of their friends. Her aunties and her uncles and all of their friends. Her cousins, little, medium and big, and all of their friends! Even Double and Trouble were there. They were noisy babies who were meant to be left at home, but they cried so much at being left behind that Anna's mother and father took pity on them and brought them along too.

Up on the stage many adults and children made long speeches of welcome. Traditional dances were performed by many schools. The big national choir sang welcome songs.

Then it was the turn of Anna Hibiscus.

Anna stood alone on the stage. On a stage big enough for a soccer game,

Anna stood alone. A sea of faces rose in front of her, but the lights shone in her eyes, and she could not see one face she knew. There was nobody standing beside her or behind her. Nobody to hold her hand or sing with her. There were only all those people looking at her; and one of those people, Anna knew, was a president from a strange and faraway country.

Anna forgot her song.

The audience was silent. Everybody
was waiting for the small girl on stage to
speak or sing or dance or do something.
The visiting president looked at her watch.

Anna Hibiscus did nothing. She did not
know her song anymore. Her throat was a
dry riverbed. Her bones had turned to stone.
She could not move. Not even to run off the
stage.

Anna Hibiscus's mother and father,
grandmother and grandfather, aunties and
uncles, cousins and friends, all looked at one
another. They held their breath and waited.

And waited.

Double was bored. He climbed up
on his chair. Trouble was bored. He too
stood up on his chair. Anna's mother and
the aunties struggled to make them sit
down. Double and Trouble could see Anna
Hibiscus standing there on the stage alone.
Double and Trouble were confused. They
were bored. They were tired. There was
only one thing to do.

"Anna 'biscus!" Trouble shouted.

"Sing!" shouted Double.

Alone on the stage, Anna Hibiscus heard
the brothers she loved shout. She looked up,
and there they were! Out in the audience,
above everybody else!

Suddenly Anna Hibiscus was not alone.
Her bones came alive. Her throat was no
longer dry. She remembered her song!
It ran like a river! Anna opened her
mouth and sang!

"Welcome to our beautiful country,
Welcome to our wonderful land.
Welcome to the sun shining brightly,
Welcome to our cool evening rain.
Welcome to our flowers always
blooming,
Welcome to our trees always green.
Welcome to our rivers of fishes,
Welcome to our farms growing food.
Welcome to our deep dark rainforest,
Welcome to our industries' sound.
Welcome to our schools full of
children,
Welcome to our cities and towns.
Welcome to our beautiful country,
Welcome to our sweet motherland!"

The audience clapped and clapped and clapped. The foreign president stood up on her feet and clapped. Anna's family and friends stood up on their feet and clapped. Everybody stood up and clapped.

"Hooray!" shouted Grandfather.

"Hooray!" shouted Grandmother.

"Hooray!" shouted her mother and father and aunties and uncles and cousins and friends and everybody else.

"Hooray! Anna 'biscus!" shouted Trouble.

"Anna 'biscus! Hooray!" shouted Double.

They were clapping the longest and
shouting the loudest.
"Hooray! Hooray! Hooray!"
It was their new word.

Your Hair, Anna Hibiscus!

Anna Hibiscus lives with her whole
entire family in Africa. Wonderful Africa.
Amazing Africa. Africa, where girls have
beautiful hair. Short or long, the hair of an
African girl is thicker and shinier and curlier
than any other hair in the whole world.

Everybody in
Anna's family must
look after their hair.
They must oil it
so that it shines
and sparkles
in the sunlight.
They must comb
it well-well.
Anna's
grandfather,
father, uncles
and boy cousins
have short-short hair.
Oil, comb, and the palaver is over. Not so
for Anna Hibiscus and her girl cousins with
their long-long hair. Not so for her aunties.
For them the headache has only just begun.

Grandmother and Grandfather say it
is best to observe the traditional African
ways, and the whole family agrees.

Traditional African women and
girls braid and weave their hair.
That is how such thick
and curly hair stays
shiny and beautiful
and neat, with
no chemicals
whatsoever.

But Anna Hibiscus
knows that braiding and weaving
mean hours and hours of hair-pulling
and head-squeezing and scalp-yanking.
Anna Hibiscus hates her hair. It is too thick;
it is too curly. Never mind that it is beautiful
and shiny. Anna Hibiscus *hates* it.

And one day Anna Hibiscus decides she
cannot stand looking after it anymore.

It was one Friday evening. Anna Hibiscus was sitting on the floor while her cousin Joy loosened all her tiny-tiny braids. Anna was uncomfortable; Anna was bored; Anna was cross. Every Friday evening was the same. Pull! Tug! Yank! The braids that had been holding her thick hair tight and neat all week had to be loosened, ready to be weaved tight and neat again the next day.

All around the room, Grandmother was helping aunties, aunties were helping big girl cousins, and big girl cousins were helping little girl cousins to loosen all the tiny-tiny tight-tight braids on each others' heads.

Anna's head was pulled first one
way and then the other. She was
getting crosser and more
uncomfortable, but
she did not dare
complain.

"Do you
see anybody else
complaining?" her aunties would ask.

Anna Hibiscus did not. Nobody else
complained. Even the smallest of small
girl cousins did not complain. They all
tried to be as brave as their mothers. But
the aunties' heads must be so hard by now,
Anna thought. After centuries of pulling
and tugging and yanking, their heads must
be as hard as concrete.

Auntie Joly combed Anna Hibiscus's loosened hair. How any knots could have entered it when it had been weaved so tightly for the whole one week, Anna

Hibiscus would never know. But knots were always there. The comb put them there on purpose.

Now it was Anna's turn to have her hair washed. Her mother's fingers were soft and gentle, rubbing her sore scalp.

Anna's hair was dried and then oiled and
then combed again. Already there
were more knots!

This thin comb would
tangle anybody's hair,
Anna Hibiscus thought
crossly.

At last one of the big cousins
put Anna's hair into thick,
easy braids to keep it
neat until
tomorrow.

Anna Hibiscus was tired of the pulling and the tugging and the yanking; and tomorrow, she knew, would be worse. Suddenly Anna Hibiscus made a decision.

Tomorrow the Saturday weaving aunties would come. Those Saturday weaving aunties who were not her aunties; who were nobodies' aunties that she knew; who she had to call auntie just to be polite. Tomorrow she would have to sit on the floor between the knees of one of those aunties. And those knees, fat or thin, those knees would grip her head firmly in place. Then the fingers of the Saturday weaving auntie would pull and pull and pull tiny fingerfuls of Anna Hibiscus's hair until Anna was surprised that her hair was not being pulled right out and falling on the ground.

And every Saturday Anna shouted and shouted because she could not help shouting

when someone was pulling out fingerfuls
of her hair. And everybody would laugh
and say, "Anna Hibiscus, you must have
a head as soft as a baby!"

Anna was furious just thinking about it.

The next morning, Grandmother and all
the aunties and the girl cousins were up
early waiting for the Saturday weaving
aunties to come and weave their hair. But
Anna Hibiscus was up even earlier. Before
the first cock crow, she peeped out of her
bedroom door, looking right, looking left.
Then she tiptoed down the corridor.

Oh no!
Here was
Grandmother!
Anna Hibiscus
flattened herself
against the wall.
Grandmother went
the other way.

Anna Hibiscus
continued to
tiptoe down
the hall.
Oh no!
Here was
Uncle Tunde!

She peeped down
the stairs. Nobody
there. Nobody except...
Oh no! Anna Hibiscus
shot back into
the corridor.
She could not
go down those
stairs without her
mother seeing her.

Anna Hibiscus tiptoed to another set of
stairs that led straight outside. She started
to go down... Oh no! Here was Uncle
Bizi Sunday! Anna Hibiscus was stuck!
The cockerel from next door flew over the
wall looking for hens and trouble. Oh no!
Now the squawking and the crowing
and the shouting would wake
everybody up!

Quick, Anna
Hibiscus ran down
the stairs, around
the corner of the
house and jumped
into the back of an
empty car. She ran all
that way and – lucky
for her – nobody saw her.
Not Grandmother, not Mother,
not Uncle Tunde, not Uncle Bizi Sunday,
not the cockerel. Only the hens saw her,
and they wouldn't tell.

Now everybody was up. Big cousins
rushed to breakfast untying their braids.
Little cousins were caught to have their hair
loosened. Aunties chose designs and held
little cousins in place and exchanged news
with the Saturday weaving aunties. Everybody was so loud and so busy that nobody
noticed – Anna Hibiscus was not there!

It was only just before they left that one of the Saturday weaving aunties asked, "Where dey de small one who like to shout?"

Grandmother, aunties and cousins looked around for Anna Hibiscus.

"It's Anna's turn to oil the little ones' hair!" complained Chocolate.

"Anna! Where have you gone?"

Suddenly everybody was asking, "Where is Anna? Where is Anna? Where has Anna Hibiscus gone?"

The big boy cousins were told to look for her high up in the fruit trees.

Chocolate and
Angel were sent to
the girls' bedrooms
to search.

Uncle Tunde
opened cupboards
and took lids off pots.
Anna's mother
texted Anna's father,
who had gone to buy
newspapers. But he did
not know where Anna
was. Anna Hibiscus
was searched for high
and low. Above and
below. Before and
behind. Inside and out.
And she was not found.

She was not found until one hour later,
when the Saturday weaving aunties had gone.

"Anna Hibiscus, what happened to you?" everybody asked.

"Ah-ah, Anna Hibiscus. We were worrying about you!" said Grandmother.

"I was asleep," said Anna. Which was true. But she did not say *where*.

"Anna Hibiscus, the Saturday weaving aunties, dey have all gone!" said Angel.

"Good!" said Anna Hibiscus.

Anna's grandmother, her mother and the aunties looked at one another.

"But what about your hair?" asked Chocolate, worried.

"I don't care."

The aunties opened their mouths wide-wide.

"Leave her," said Grandmother. "She will learn."

I will, thought Anna happily. I will learn how to do my hair properly without all that pulling and tugging and yanking.

50

Anna Hibiscus was very proud of herself. She had made a decision and carried it out.

That night, before eating, Anna loosened her thick braids and put her hair into two neat pompoms. She tied the pompoms with ribbons. It took about two minutes, and Anna Hibiscus felt very pretty, and very, very happy.

At bedtime, Anna Hibiscus refused to take out the pompoms and put the thick braids back in.

"Leave her," said Grandmother again.

The next morning, Anna Hibiscus's
pompoms were squashed and full of knots.

Anna Hibiscus went to her mother and
father's room. She put her father's softening
oil on her hair and tried to brush out the knots
with her mother's soft brush. The brush stuck
fast. Anna had to pull the brush to get it out
of her hair. She had to pull it hard. "Ow!"
Anna shaped the knotty pompoms with
her fingers and went downstairs.

Grandfather sent her back upstairs.
"You can't go to church like that," he said.

Anna found a pretty head tie
to cover her squashed and
knotty pompoms.

"Tomorrow is
school," said Cousin
Clarity. "You can't go
to school with your
hair in a head tie.
It's not allowed."

On Monday morning, Anna Hibiscus took out the squashed and knotty pompoms and tried to smooth her hair with her hands before she went downstairs. Little cousins looked at her sticking-up-and-out hair with big eyes. Big cousins looked with worried eyes. Anna's mother, aunties and uncles and grandmother looked away.

Nobody offered to help Anna Hibiscus, and Anna Hibiscus did not ask for anybody's help. No more pulling and tugging and yanking from them. No, thank you!

At school the other children laughed at Anna Hibiscus's hair, but Anna Hibiscus pretended not to care.

Anna's hair grew worse and worse. Every night more and more knots jumped into her hair, and every morning it was more and more impossible to comb.

On Tuesday morning Anna Hibiscus spent a long time alone with her father's comb. But the knots would not budge. She cried as she tried to comb out the knots and tangles. She cried as she pulled and tugged and yanked her own hair. She cried when the children at school teased her.

On Wednesday morning she took the comb to her mother.

"Oh, Anna!" her mother sighed.

Anna's mother tried to help, but Anna's mother's hair was straight; she did not know a lot about curly hair. The little girl cousins tried

to help: they pulled
and tugged and
yanked. But it was
no use. Anna Hibiscus's
hair was one big knot.

On Thursday
morning the teacher
said, "Anna Hibiscus,
go home and come back
when you do not look
so disgraceful."

Anna Hibiscus
did not tell anybody
what the teacher
said. But on Friday
morning she hid.

After the other cousins had gone to school, Grandmother came to find Anna. Anna's hair was still thicker and curlier than any hair anywhere in the world, but it was no longer shiny and beautiful. It was rough and dry and sticking up in every place.

"Come with me, Anna Hibiscus," said Grandmother. "Let me help you now."

Grandmother rubbed thick grease in Anna's hair to soften it. She wet it to loosen the knots. She spent a long time softly, softly loosening the knots with her gentle fingers. Then she had to pull and tug and yank with the comb, but Anna did not complain. She was grateful to Grandmother for helping her. Some of the knots were so tight that Grandmother had to cut them out with scissors. Tears rolled down Anna's face as she saw her beautiful hair fall to the ground. But she did not shout.

"Anna Hibiscus, your hair! It is short now!" cried the other girl cousins when they saw her.

But Anna Hibiscus did not care. Her problems were over. Grandmother had loosened them and cut them all out.

Anna Hibiscus was happy. Tomorrow the Saturday weaving aunties would come. They would weave her hair into short but beautiful braids. Braids that would stay on her head for one whole week, not causing any trouble, not requiring any combing, pulling, tugging or yanking! No more teasing or worrying or hiding. Anna Hibiscus would be able to hold her head high all week!

Saturday came and, for the first time
ever, Anna Hibiscus did not shout even
one shout.

No, while her hair was pulled and
tugged and yanked in tiny fingerfuls,
Anna Hibiscus smiled.

Anna Hibiscus and the New Generator

Anna Hibiscus lives in Africa. Amazing Africa. She lives with her whole family in a big white house in a beautiful garden in the middle of a big compound.

Like every other family in Africa, the evening is a busy time for Anna's family. Clothes must be washed and rinsed and hung up to dry. Food must be prepared while it is still light.

"Change your clothes!" shouts Auntie Joly at the cousins returning from school.

"Come and pound yam!" calls Anna's mother when she gets home from work.

Anna Hibiscus runs to loose Double from her mother's back. She is too small to pound yam, but she is big enough to look after Double, and she is big enough to wash her school clothes ready for the next day.

Food is cooked and eaten and cleared away. It is now dark outside. But in the lit-up house, there is still a lot going on.

The bright and shining house is full of noise. The air conditioners are loud, and the television is even louder. Small cousins are crying and whining because they are tired and do not want to go to bed. Double and Trouble whine the loudest of all.

Even outside on the veranda the radio is talking and singing above the voices of the uncles. Only Grandmother and Grandfather are still and quiet, dozing in a corner. Soon

Double and Trouble will crawl onto their soft laps and fall asleep.

One night Anna Hibiscus and her cousins were watching television; aunties were sewing on noisy machines; big cousins were homeworking under bright lights; uncles were arguing with the radio.

Suddenly the lights went out! The radio and television were quenched. The air conditioners and sewing machines fell silent.

Electricity was gone!

This is quite normal in Africa. If electricity is there, it is there. If it is gone, it is gone. No point asking questions. That is how it is in Africa. Everything is unpredictable. You can count on it.

Now it was **DARK**. Now it was **QUIET**. Anna Hibiscus could see nothing. But she could hear her heart pounding in her chest. She could hear the frogs croak and the mosquitoes whine. She could hear the slap of the lagoon water on the city's dry banks and the roar of the cars in the dark streets. It was dark. It was quiet. It was wonderful!

For a moment, nobody moved, not an inch, not uncles or aunties or cousins. Nobody moved except for Grandmother and Grandfather. They sat bolt upright. Awake! Double and Trouble shuffled on their laps. Then suddenly aunties and uncles and big cousins were calling and searching for matches and candles and flashlights. Double and Trouble rubbed their eyes.

Anna Hibiscus jumped up and down and yelled, "Hooray! Hooray!"

Little cousins ran shouting. Chocolate and Angel played hide-and-seek in the candlelight and dark. Double and Trouble looked around with big, wide eyes at the deep shadows and the dancing yellow candles and the beams of white flashlight. Grandfather made a cool breeze with his fan. It was wonderful.

The big cousins came downstairs. They had to do their homework at the table by the light of the paraffin lamp. Aunties drifted out to talk with uncles on the veranda. There were jokes and laughing. The uncles teased the aunties with songs, and the aunties laughed and danced and softly clapped their hands. The swish-swish of Grandfather's fan joined in.

Then Grandmother told a story. The
homework stopped; the jokes and the
dancing and the songs stopped. The whole
family gathered to listen to Grandmother.
Even Double and Trouble sat quietly. One
by one the little cousins fell asleep. When
Grandmother's stories stopped they would
be carried by flashlight to bed. Through
the screens of the open bedroom windows,
the songs of the frogs and the lagoon would
last throughout the night. Wonderful!

One evening Anna's father and the uncles said, "We have an announcement! We have bought a generator. Now when the electricity fails we will still have light!"

The big cousins shouted happily; the aunties exclaimed loudly; Grandmother and Grandfather looked interested. Anna Hibiscus was excited. What did this mean?

Men came with a truck. A big machine was unloaded and stationed underneath Anna Hibiscus's favorite mango tree. Anna started to look worried.

Two evenings later, the lights went out.
The air conditioners and sewing machines and
radio and television fell silent. It was dark. It
was quiet. It was wonderful. Grandmother and
Grandfather sat up. Double and Trouble stirred.
The frogs croaked; the lagoon sang. The uncles
ran outside to turn on the generator.

A huge engine noise was heard, and the lights
came back on! The rooms were bright and the
television loud again. Cheers and shouts were
heard from every corner of the house.

The cousins continued with their homework
upstairs. They had not even had time
to come down. Aunties who were starting
to joke went back to their television
and sewing machines. Triumphant
uncles congratulated each other
and went back to the radio on the
veranda. Double and Trouble
started to cry. Anna Hibiscus

and the little cousins looked sadly at one
another. There had been no flashlight or
candles. There had been no hide-and-seek.

Anna could see Grandmother and
Grandfather in the corner. They looked
small and old. Grandmother started to
say something, but nobody heard her. The
noise of the generator and the televisions
and the radio and the air conditioners
and the sewing machines was too loud.
Grandmother went back to sleep. The
story she would have told was gone.

Grandfather had lifted his fan ready to cool himself, but the air conditioners were already back on. Slowly, he lowered it. He looked sadly at Anna Hibiscus and Double and Trouble.

Double and Trouble cried and cried until they were taken upstairs to bed. They were confused; they were upset.

Now, every day, the uncles were out with the new generator. Polishing it and oiling it and tightening it up with tools. Double and Trouble and all the cousins, little, medium and big, watched – but they were not allowed to touch.

The new generator was right underneath Anna Hibiscus's favorite mango tree. Now whenever she came out to climb her tree, it was full of big cousins looking down at the generator. It was crowded with uncles and little cousins admiring the generator.

It was busy with friends
come to congratulate the
uncles. The ground was
littered with tools and
oil and rags.

Anna Hibiscus sucked her
teeth! This is what you do in Africa when
you are not at all happy with somebody …
or something. Anna Hibiscus sucked her
teeth again. What was that machine doing
underneath her tree? What was it doing
in her compound at all? It had come and
swallowed Grandmother's stories, and the
songs of the frogs and the lagoon. It had
come and blown out the candlelight and the
flashlight and the jokes of the aunties and
uncles. It had come and stolen the games
little cousins played in the dark. It had filled
the wide eyes of babies full of tears.

Anna Hibiscus did not like the generator
at-all at-all.

There was somebody else who did not like that generator. Somebody else who knew it was in the way. Pronto, the old he-goat with the long, strong horns. Pronto liked to scratch his back on the very same branch the generator stood beneath. Now the generator was blocking the branch.

One day, at last, the uncles and cousins were busy with something else, their friends had gone home, and the aunties had returned to their work. Anna Hibiscus climbed her tree alone, in peace. But the generator was still there. Pronto was chewing and glaring at it.

Suddenly the generator *twanged*! It *wanged* and it *clanged*! Anna Hibiscus clung to her branch and looked down. The generator was alive!

Pronto stared at the generator. His rival had spoken. Pronto rammed the big machine with his long, strong horns. If ever a younger he-goat were to walk into the compound, Pronto would deal with him just so.

He butted it hard again and again. The generator *clanged* and *twanged* and *shouted*! Anna was frozen on her branch. She did not know what to do!

The old goat
was strong, but the
generator did not
move one inch.
Pronto gave up
and walked off
stiffly. He had
not yet succeeded
in driving his rival away, but
at least he had taught him a lesson.

The generator was silent. A tool came
flying out from behind it. The tool was
followed first by Trouble and then by
Double. Anna Hibiscus's mouth fell open!
It had been Double and Trouble *twanging*
and *wanging* the generator!

Anna Hibiscus stayed up in the tree for
a long time, thinking. She decided to say
nothing. She climbed down.

The next time the electricity went off and the uncles came to switch on the generator, it would not start. There was no joking or laughing or dancing that night. The aunties sat sighing at their silent sewing machines. Big cousins stared at each other over their homework. Only the little cousins were happy; only Grandmother and Grandfather were content; only Double and Trouble rubbed their eyes and smiled.

The uncles called a mechanic, but there was nothing he could do. The generator

was broken. Kaput. Anna Hibiscus's mother and father, her aunties and uncles and all the big cousins were very sad.

Anna Hibiscus could not stop thinking about Double and Trouble and the generator and Pronto ramming it, and herself up in the tree saying nothing and still saying nothing now! Anna Hibiscus could not stop thinking, but she did not know what to do.

Grandmother and Grandfather noticed. They noticed that when the lights went out, Anna Hibiscus no longer shouted "Hooray!" She no longer laughed and ran and played hide-and-seek.

One day when the house was quiet and empty, they called her.

"What is the matter, Anna Hibiscus?" Grandfather asked.

"Nothing, Grandfather," replied Anna.

"Are you missing the generator?" Grandmother asked gently.

Anna burst into tears.

Grandmother and Grandfather looked
at each other. Anna Hibiscus told them the
whole story. She told them how the generator
had come alive and how Pronto had rammed
it, and how a tool had come flying out from
behind it followed by Double and Trouble.

Grandmother and Grandfather laughed
and laughed. They could not stop. Double
and Trouble crawled over to join in the fun.
They did not know why Grandmother and
Grandfather were laughing, but they wanted
to laugh too.

"Hooray!" shouted
Double happily.

Now Anna started
to laugh. She could not
help herself. Grandmother
and Grandfather, Anna
Hibiscus, and Double
and Trouble laughed
and laughed.

That night, when the whole family was gathered to eat, Grandfather made an announcement.

"Generators," said Grandfather, "are very un-traditional. They are guzzlers of money. They are destroyers of the peace. God has ordained some nights for modern, busy noisiness, and others for more traditional pursuits. God gives us electricity some nights and takes it away other nights. This is a balance between modern and traditional. Our family will spend no more money on disturbing this balance. No more generators in this compound!"

Anna Hibiscus breathed a sigh of relief. Now she need not say anything about Double and Trouble and Pronto and the generator to anybody else. They had probably been acting under Grandfather's orders. Or God's.

That night, in the dark and quiet,
Grandmother's stories were about
an old he-goat, troublesome but wise!

The Other
Side of the City

Anna Hibiscus lives with her mother
and her father; her grandmother and her
grandfather; her aunties and their husbands;
her uncles and their wives; all her many,
many cousins; and her two baby brothers.
They all live together in a big white house
in a large, quiet compound in a huge, busy
city in the middle of a wonderful country
on the amazing continent of Africa.

The city that Anna Hibiscus lives in is full
of roads and lagoons, full of cars and boats, full
of people. Poor people and rich people, all rush
and hurry. Anna's compound is quiet – much
quieter than the busy-busy city outside the
gate with its millions of people and thousands
of roads and hundreds of lagoons.

Anna Hibiscus often looks through
the gate to the lagoon on the other side of
the road. It is crowded with boats coming
and going from the other side of the city.

"Come and play, Anna Hibiscus,"
said Cousin Sweetheart one day.

"Why are you always looking outside?"
asked Cousin Joy.

Anna wanted to go on the ferry across
the lagoon. Anna wanted to see the other
side of the city. That was why she was
always looking and looking.

"What can there be to see?" said Cousin
Wonderful. "It can only be more houses like
this. More people like us."

But still Anna wanted to go. Still Anna
had to see.

Uncle Bizi Sunday
often went on one
of those lagoon
ferry boats.
Uncle Bizi
Sunday had
people he went
to see on the other side of the city.
Anna Hibiscus decided to ask him, again.

"Stop troubling me!" said Uncle
Bizi Sunday.

Auntie Joly also
went to the other side
of the city. She took
clothes sometimes
to a home for
motherless babies
there. Anna
decided to ask her.

"Anna Hibiscus," Auntie Joly sighed, "why do you want to go to the other side of the city? The people there are poor. It is not a good place. The other side of the city has nothing to do with you."

So Anna Hibiscus asked Uncle Tunde and her other uncles.

She asked Auntie Grace and her other aunties.

They all said the same thing. "It is a poor place. It is not a good place. Why does it concern you?"

Anna asked Grandmother and Grandfather, "Is it bad to be poor? Is it wrong?"

"No," said Grandmother. "It is not bad. It is not wrong. But it is not easy to be very poor."

"It is not easy to look at poverty either," Anna's mother added.

"It is not nice to be very poor, and it is not nice to see, Anna Hibiscus," said her father. "The other side of the city is not for you."

But still Anna Hibiscus wanted to go.

"Let her go," said Grandfather. "Let her see; let her know."

Anna Hibiscus jumped up and down! Hooray! Hooray! She was going on a ferry. She was going to cross the lagoon. She was going to see the other side of the city!

"Thank you, Grandfather! Thank you!" she shouted, and ran to tell Sweetheart and Joy and Wonderful and all the other cousins.

"Let her see and know just how lucky she is," said Grandfather, sighing.

Anna Hibiscus got ready. She oiled her neatly braided hair. She chose her best pink Sunday dress, her favorite hair ribbons and her new Sunday shoes.

"Remove the shoes," said Auntie Joly. "Do you want to spoil them in the boat?"

Anna Hibiscus put her shoes back in the cupboard. She put on her old pink flip-flops. All flip-flops Anna's size were pink. Other sizes were other colors.

Auntie Joly and Uncle Bizi Sunday were
going to take Anna on the ferry. Auntie Joly
wore one of her old dresses; Uncle Bizi
Sunday wore his working clothes. Only
Anna Hibiscus looked pretty and smart.
Grandmother sighed when she saw her.
But she didn't say why.

Down by the lagoon there were many, many people all pushing and squeezing and rushing to get on and off the ferry. Anna Hibiscus held tight to Uncle Bizi Sunday's hand. A man with strong legs was keeping the ferry in place. He had one foot on the jetty and one foot in the ferry. Auntie Joly jumped onto the ferry. Uncle Bizi Sunday jumped onto the ferry. Anna Hibiscus had to jump too. She had to jump if she wanted to go to the other side of the city.

Uncle Bizi Sunday held out his arms to Anna Hibiscus. As Anna jumped, a big woman jumped too, bumping Anna and rocking the ferry. Anna almost fell into the lagoon, but Uncle Bizi Sunday caught her arm quick-quick and pulled her into the boat. One of Anna Hibiscus's pink flip-flops fell into the lagoon. It floated away with the rest of the rubbish under the boat and was gone.

"Do you want to kill my brother's child?"
Auntie Joly shouted. "Wha' kind of woman
are you? Ca' you not see a child when she
is jumping in front of you?"

Quickly the woman said, "Sorry, ma. Sorry."
She looked at Anna Hibiscus. "Don' cry.
Don' cry," she said.

Anna Hibiscus could not stop crying. She had almost fallen into the lagoon. Her arm was hurting where Uncle Bizi Sunday had pulled her into the boat. Her dress was dirty, and one of her flip-flops was lost forever.

"Don' cry!" said Uncle Bizi Sunday. "You are not the only one without shoes."

Anna Hibiscus looked. Most of the people on the ferry had no shoes. Their bare feet

rested in the rubbish and the dirty water
in the bottom of the boat. Just like Anna's
one bare foot.

Anna stopped crying. She kept on her
other flip-flop. What else could she do? Anna
Hibiscus worried. Would people on the other
side of the city notice her beautiful dress
and her pretty ribbons and her shiny hair,
or would they only notice her one shoe?

The overloaded ferry reached the other side of the lagoon, and Uncle Bizi Sunday carried Anna Hibiscus down from the boat. Anna looked around.

The first person she saw was a beggar girl holding her hands out for coins. Her hair was ragged and matted into dusty, dirty clumps. She had no legs.

The beggar girl looked at Anna Hibiscus and called out, "Fine girl, help me. Fine girl, help your sister!"

Anna Hibiscus did not know what to do. She did not want to look at the beggar girl with no legs. She had no money to help this new "sister" who was like no other girl she had seen before, rich or poor. So Anna hid behind Auntie Joly until they had moved away.

Now Anna Hibiscus could look again.
All around were many, many
people wearing torn and faded
clothes. The roads were
narrow, and the gutters
stank like toilets. There
were many, many houses
all squeezed together.
One-room houses made
of old, rotting wood and
rusty, corrugated iron
patched with cardboard
boxes. Among them
were big piles of rotting
rubbish. The sound
of babies crying
and people
shouting filled
the air.

Anna Hibiscus had never seen anything like this before. She wanted to close her eyes and close her nose and close her ears and make it all go away, but her eyes and nose and ears stayed open and wide. She held tight to Auntie Joly's hand.

Auntie Joly and Uncle Bizi Sunday stopped outside a one-room house made of corrugated iron full of rusty holes. A weak voice called for them to enter. It was hot inside. The sun beat down on the iron walls and roof, heating the room like an oven. It was too hot for Anna Hibiscus.

"Anna Hibiscus, go and wait for us outside," Auntie Joly said, after she had greeted the sick, old woman lying on a mat.

Outside, it was not so hot. The sun still beat down, but there was air. Close to Anna Hibiscus was a pile of rubbish. A big pile of rubbish. There were children climbing all over it.

Anna went closer. The children were naked or clothed in rags. They were picking things out of the rubbish. They were *eating* the rubbish!

Anna Hibiscus could not blink or even think. Suddenly she no longer knew why she was wearing her best pink Sunday dress and her favorite ribbons. She hoped none of the children would notice, or they would know she did not have to eat rubbish. They would know she had pretty dresses while they ate rubbish.

Anna Hibiscus saw one girl, dressed only in ragged underpants, pick a flip-flop out of the rubbish. It was pink. The same as Anna's. The girl tried it on. It fitted. She was the same size as Anna Hibiscus!

The girl saw Anna Hibiscus watching her. They looked at each other, and the girl frowned. Anna Hibiscus was wearing her best pink dress. She had pretty ribbons in her hair. The girl was wearing ragged gray underpants. Her hair was all cut off. But they were both wearing only one pink flip-flop. Anna Hibiscus smiled at the girl. The girl gave Anna Hibiscus a crooked smile back.

Slowly, Anna Hibiscus took off her one pink flip-flop. She held it out to the girl.

106

The girl shook her head and frowned.
So Anna Hibiscus put her flip-flop on the
pile of rubbish and turned her back on it.
Quickly, before anyone else could, the girl
picked up the flip-flop and put it on.

Anna Hibiscus looked around and saw the
girl skipping away down the street in her
matching pink flip-flops. Anna gazed at the
other naked, ragged children. She thought of
her many dresses hanging in the cupboard
in her room. And Anna Hibiscus took off her
dress. She took it off right there in the street
and threw it onto
the rubbish heap.

When Auntie Joly and
Uncle Bizi Sunday
came out, Anna
Hibiscus was waiting
for them. She looked
almost like the other
children. Except she was
clean and so were her white
pants, and she also had
ribbons in her hair.

"Way-tin happen?"
Uncle Bizi Sunday cried.

"Anna Hibiscus!" shouted Auntie Joly.
"What kind of nonsense is this?"

Anna Hibiscus did not answer. She was
watching a small girl dancing down the road
in a pink Sunday dress. She looked at Auntie
Joly and Uncle Bizi Sunday and smiled her
biggest smile.

Auntie Joly gasped and closed her eyes. Uncle Bizi Sunday shook his head. "Anna Hibiscus!" he said.

"Grandmother will deal with you at home, Anna Hibiscus," Auntie Joly said, and she led her back to the ferry.

The beggar girl was still there by the jetty. She saw Anna Hibiscus. Anna did not look so fine now. But she was feeling better than before. She took her favorite ribbons from her hair and tied them softly, softly in the matted hair of the beggar girl with no legs.

The beggar girl looked at Anna Hibiscus with wide eyes. "God bless you!" she whispered.

And that is exactly what Grandmother said
after Anna Hibiscus explained to the gathered
family why she had come home in only
her underpants.

"Hooray!" said Double.

"Hooray for Anna 'biscus!"
said Trouble.

Atinuke was born in Nigeria
and spent her childhood in both Africa
and the UK. Before writing her first book,
Anna Hibiscus, she worked internationally
as a storyteller, telling tales from both Africa
and the African Diaspora. Her stories are
a medley of traditional folklore and
contemporary urban life. Set in the Africa
of her childhood, *Hooray for Anna Hibiscus!*
is her second book. Atinuke lives with her
husband and two young sons in Wales.

Lauren Tobia always enjoyed
drawing as a child. When she grew up she
worked as an intensive care nurse for many
years before taking a foundation course
and gaining a degree in illustration at
the University of the West of England,
Bristol. *Anna Hibiscus* was her first children's
book. Lauren lives in Bristol with her
husband, two daughters and her
three-legged greyhound, Mickey.